THE MIDNIGHT *Marquess*

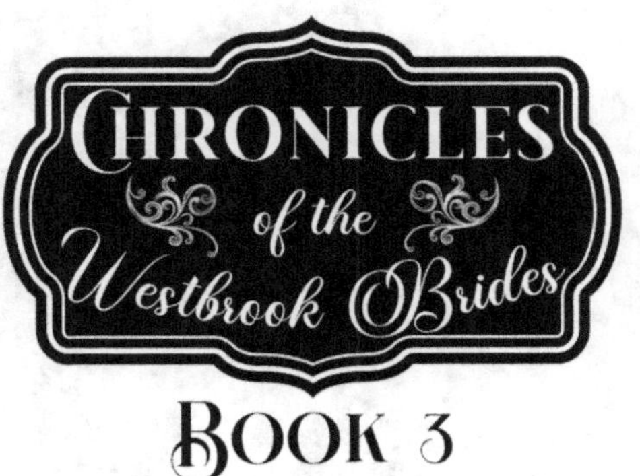

CHRONICLES of the Westbrook Brides

BOOK 3

USA *Today* Bestselling Author

COLLETTE CAMERON®

SWEET-TO-SPICY TIMELESS ROMANCE ®

Blue Rose Romance® LLC

"Would you like to come for tea tomorrow?" she asked.

Would he?

Did whales swim?

Did hawks fly?

Did the sun rise every morning?

Attn: Permissions Coordinator

Blue Rose Romance® LLC

PO Box 167

Scappoose, Oregon 97056 USA

collettecameron.com

eBook ISBN: 9781955259514

Print Book ISBN: 978-1-955259-75-0

USA Today Bestselling Author
Sweet to Spicy Timeless Romance®
COLLETTE
collettecameron.com
CAMERON®
Blue Rose Romance® LLC

PRAISE FOR...
THE MIDNIGHT MARQUESS©

See What Readers Are Saying About
The Midnight Marquess!

★★★★★ "I adored this story for it's simplicity and how we sometimes tend to agonize over a situation that only exists in our minds. A truly lovely story that makes us believe in love at first sight."

— GHAZAL

★ ★ ★ ★ ★ "*The Midnight Marquess* is a charming and heartwarming tale of love, trust, and forgiveness that will make you swoon and smile. The characters were so likable, and I loved Antoinette, the cat, who made their "cute meet" possible!"

— LANA BIRKY

★★★★★ "Sweet read with not only delightful characters, but add children, a spoiled cat and puppies! How could it not be a win/win?"

— LINDA J

★★★★★ "An enchanting sweet story, with all the wonderful characters, including the four legged kind, that this author is such a master at creating!"

— LORI D

★★★★★ "What an absolutely sweet book. Well written, fast paced, full of drama, love, romance, action, fabulous characters and a superb storyline. The author keeps your attention and brings you to the end wanting more."

— ROSE SEALS

THE MIDNIGHT MARQUESS

A ROMANTIC OPPOSITES ATTRACT MYSTERY &
SUSPENSE FAMILY SAGA REGENCY ROMANCE

CHRONICLES OF THE WESTBROOK BRIDES
BOOK THREE

COLLETTE CAMERON®

GET YOUR FREE BOOK!

THE REGENCY ROSE®

VIP CLUB

Acknowledgments

Thank you, Joanna D'Angelo and Dee Foster for all your hard work. You are invaluable! I don't know what I would do without you!

ONE

Lymington, New Forest
Hampshire, England
Number 16 Harbor View Lane

LATE APRIL 1826 – JUST PAST MIDNIGHT

A superior French cognac dangling from the fingers of one hand, Adolphus Westbrook slung his ankle across his knee as he leaned his head back against the chaise longue's cushion and observed the glittering diamond-like stars in the backdrop of the black-as-coal sky.

The cottage's open lower-story windows glowed golden behind lace panels—inviting and soothing. An eight-foot-high brick wall encased the small square rear lawn and garden, preventing inquisitive neighbors from intruding into his private oasis or peeking into the house's ground floor.

Tangy with salt and sea, a balmy breeze better suited to the tropics than the English coast teased the leaves with a lover's gentle caress. Coatless, his shirt unbuttoned and the sleeves rolled to his elbows, Adolphus wiggled his stockinged toes sans his boots.

Seymour, his valet in London, would be profoundly and utterly appalled at the breach of etiquette—which was precisely why the manservant remained in the city.

My little slice of heaven.

Adolphus sighed, allowing the tension to slip away as he relaxed and enjoyed the quiet and solace of his favorite time of day. No pressures or expectations. No duties or responsibilities demanded the immediate attention of the Marquess of Edenhaven, future Duke of Latham. There was no one to raise a censorial eyebrow at his dishabille or frown at stockinged feet, tousled hair, and bristly jaw.

Of more import—*God save me*—there were no marriage-minded *le beau monde* mamas and their doe-eyed, nincompoop daughters to avoid, and—*praise the saints*—no frivolous young bucks with more virility than brains to put in their places with a scathing glare.

Had he ever been so codpated and bacon-brained? Ruled entirely by his libido?

Assuredly not—more was the pity.

At Christmastide he'd decided it was time to search for a wife, a woman like his sister Althelia. Except, Adolphus hadn't met any women like her, and he'd made no real effort to look either. Years of avoiding grasping duchess want-to-bees couldn't be unlearned overnight and neither could his pessimism and cynicism when it came to women.

Adolphus took a sip of cognac, holding it in his mouth for a couple of seconds, savoring the robust flavor and velvety texture before swallowing. The mellow heat glided to his stomach, coating his insides with warmth.

Not that he needed warming.

The sunniest area in all of England and possessing the mildest clime, Lymington might not be a sultry Caribbean or Mediterranean paradise, but the temperate evening proved quite refreshing and tranquil.

Yes, purchasing this inconspicuous cottage in the rustic borough last year had been just the thing. Adolphus hadn't intended to buy property in the coastal township. However, on a visit to check on his investments, he'd given into a rare impulse and purchased the furnished house, tended by a cook-housekeeper, a maid, and a man of all work.

Lymington, a quaint harbor township established in the second century and boasting Georgian influence, had become his escape and reprieve from London's stench, noise, hubbub, and the never-ending demands a peer of the realm faced. And don't forget evading matrimonial-minded denizens intent on securing a title for their eager daughters, the ilk of which infested London's Marriage Mart as numerous as vermin in London's rookeries.

His motives weren't all self-serving. He'd invested in the thriving salt industry in the area and had a vested interest in no less than three ships undergoing construction near the town quay, so residing in Lymington part of the time made perfect sense.

However, the residents knew him simply as Ab Westbrook, not a wealthy marquess and future duke. And Adolphus wanted to remain anonymous. He relished the anonymity and convenience of being an ordinary man. Many people who would've typically fawned at his feet could scarcely be bothered to spare him a glance or give him the time of day in Lymington.

Adolphus didn't mind the obscurity a jot.

True, a chance existed that someone would recognize him—a visitor, a tourist, a local he'd yet to meet—but for now, he'd maintain his false persona. He'd derived his alias, Ab, from the first letter of his given name and of one of his middle names, Benedict.

His family wasn't even aware he owned this sanctuary —mightn't ever know, truth be told. During a moment of insanity in March while visiting his childhood home, Hefferwickshire House—the ducal grand estate—he'd nearly blurted the truth to them. But something precious and private had held the impulse in check.

This cottage and township were *his* treasures.

He needn't share them with anyone else—not even the duchy.

Besides, on Adolphus's last visit home, his brother Lucius had provided enough excitement and distraction by arriving with a mysterious Spanish beauty. Clodovea had piqued Adolphus's interest, but when he realized Lucius was tail-feathers-over-beak besotted with Miss de Soverosa, Adolphus had done the gentlemanly thing and retreated.

He'd not risk alienating another brother over a woman —even if she were an intriguing, intelligent, sultry incomparable.

Last Christmas, he and his adopted brother Layton had made significant progress toward amending the rift between them. Nevertheless, Adolphus had learned his lesson through and through. Though Virginia, Layton's dead wife, had been a harlot at heart and propositioned everything in trousers, Adolphus had resolved to stay well away from his brothers' women and never again offer unsolicited advice.

It seemed a man in love was incapable of seeing what was before his nose.

Adolphus wrangled his wayward musings back to the present and his main reason for being in Lymington—in particular, this neat cottage situated on a sloping cobbled street.

His birthright had dictated his entire future since he came squalling into the world three and thirty years ago. This cottage in a respectable, if not precisely affluent and elite, neighborhood was his lone bit of rebellion from the life imposed upon him.

He couldn't travel as he yearned to, unfettered and free, so he did the next best thing.

Built ships.

Glorious, sleek vessels that would sail to all the exotic and fascinating ports he longed to visit and explore but never would.

A future duke wasn't permitted the privilege of galivanting about the world as Adolphus's brothers, Lucius, Leonidas, Darius, his twin Cassius, and Layton, were wont to do. Even their sister, Althelia had spent a couple of years in America whilst Adolphus stayed with his boots planted firmly on good ol' English soil.

Heaven forbid that the ducal heir should become ill, get injured, or, God's toenails, *die* while roving from country to country or sailing the seven seas.

Both of which had been cherished boyhood dreams.

Oh, the grand adventures Adolphus had planned, the explorations and escapades he'd imagined, the quests he'd meant to accomplish.

Before the reality of his birth and position had shoved

those unrealistic fantasies overboard to sink to the bottom of the ocean. To lay like sunken treasure, never to be retrieved. Even if said future duke had several brothers who could easily take his place should the worst occur.

But the worse wouldn't because, though no saint, Adolphus knew his duty.

Hadn't it been drilled into him since he could walk and talk? Until at the ripe young age of six, he'd comprehended his life with its privileges wasn't truly his own.

The duchy always had and always would dictate his choices and future, and it always, *always*, came first. Not sailing vessels to foreign destinations nor traipsing through humid jungles or trekking across scorching deserts.

Skewing his mouth into a mocking grin, Adolphus narrowed his eyes, angled his head, and studied the jumble of stars overhead. He was absolute rot at identifying constellations. Some ship's captain he would've made.

He squinted.

Was that group of stars Leo?

It could be Pegasus or a pig, for all he knew.

Ah, well.

He hitched a shoulder before taking a hefty swig of cognac.

In truth, other than the Milky Way and the Plough, he had no idea where one constellation ended and another began. Such studies were not part of proper peerage tutelage, yet any smuggler worth his salt would know exactly where he was at sea based on the stars' location.

Cocking an eyebrow, Adolphus gave the amber liquid in his tumbler a speculative glance. Might this have been smugglers' contraband not so long ago?

Lymington had a robust and fascinating smuggling history. Supposedly, clandestine tunnels beneath the streets led to the harbor. Rumor had it that a former Church of St. Thomas vicar had allowed smugglers to store contraband in the church's tower—no doubt for a percentage of the booty. Or so the locals proudly claimed without a hint of compunction or chagrin.

"Get down here, you pesky creature."

A woman's husky whisper caused Adolphus to lift his head and turn toward her frantic French-accented murmurs coming from the yard beyond the brick barrier.

"*Zut*, rotten cat," she muttered. "Spoiled. Cosseted. Pampered. *Mon Dieu*. You cause me no end of trouble."

Atop the brick wall dividing his cottage from the one next door, as nonchalant as a lion basking in the African sun, lay a long-haired white cat flicking its bushy tail. The feline gazed at Adolphus with an imperious *who-are-you* stare befitting a queen.

He'd not met any of his neighbors—by deliberate choice —but neither had anyone occupied that particular house on the other occasions Adolphus had been in Lymington.

When had they opened the cottage?

Of more import and concern, were the occupants here to stay, and would they disturb his peaceful retreat?

Movement and more mumbling echoed from the garden wall's other side.

If Adolphus had to guess, the woman dragged a chair to the edge to retrieve her cat.

Adolphus caught a whiff of honeysuckle carried on the balmy night air. It must be from next door, for his little strip of land didn't contain the plant.

Clearly of no mind to obey its mistress, the creature stood and then arched its spine.

"*Non*. You shall not jump. I have no wish to climb over the wall," the woman whispered with such vehemence Adolphus couldn't suppress a grin. "I do not know the neighbor, but I'm sure whoever they are, they would not appreciate a midnight visitor. Besides, I might break a leg. Not that you would care."

The cat deigned to give her a haughty glance before, with a swish of its considerable tail, lifted a front paw and licked it.

Had the good Lord ever created a creature more arrogant, entitled, and disdainful than cats?

Adolphus grinned.

Why, yes, He had.

English aristocrats, and he was related to several. Not

his immediate family, of course. Those Westbrooks didn't put on airs.

More irritated muttering continued in French and filtered to him on the night breeze.

After setting his tumbler aside, he rose and glanced around the garden. He hadn't a ladder or other chair to stand upon, and the chaise longue wasn't tall enough to do much good.

He spied a rake tucked into a corner by a small shed, along with a few other garden tools.

Raising an eyebrow, he gave the self-satisfied cat a side-eyed glance.

The feline would not like Adolphus's solution to the dilemma.

"Come down here this minute, Antoinette. You selfish beast. I am tired and must be out of bed by six. *Zut.* You can sleep all day, but I cannot. Do you know how late it is?"

Or early.

It must be close to one in the morning.

Fatigue even weighted Adolphus's eyelids, and he smothered a yawn.

The woman changed her tone, weariness replacing her vexation.

"*S'il te plait,* Antoinette."

What did she expect when she'd named the cat after a cossetted queen?

Pity for the fatigued woman stirred him, for surely it wasn't her beguiling voice and seductive accent that caused the ripple of awareness thrumming through him.

Adolphus grabbed the rake before stealthily approaching the partition.

"I might be able to help."

Absolute silence met his offer.

Craning his neck, he regarded the cat, still intent on grooming herself. In the moonlight, her white coat took on a silvery glow.

Were her eyes blue or green?

"Hello? Are you still there?" he asked.

"*Oui*," came a tentative response.

"I cannot quite reach her and have nothing to stand on. I do have a rake. Do you think she'll jump down if I gently nudge her?"

A low, derisive but very fetching chuckle met his inquiry.

"*Oui*, but she won't like it and may never forgive you. Antoinette holds grudges. And I should warn you, she gets even."

Excellent.

Mayhap the pampered puss would stay off the wall in the future.

"I'll take that chance."

However, before Adolphus could prod the cat, she

turned, lifted her tail in a rude feline snub, and hopped down.

More rustling ensued, followed by a cat's plaintive yowl.

"*S' monsieur.* I have her now. I am sorry to have inconvenienced you."

"Think nothing of it."

Adolphus propped the rake against the bricks before leaning a shoulder on the cold, hard surface and folding his arms. He'd never know what the devil prompted him to add, "Sleep well. Sweet dreams."

Too much cognac.

That was what.

"*Merci. Bonne nuit.*"

"Good night."

The mysterious woman's dulcet tones lingered with Adolphus long after he climbed into his bed and stared at the ceiling with his hands folded beneath his head.

Who was his midnight visitor?

Why did he care?

TWO

Near Candle Glow Cottage
Number 18 Harbor View Lane
Lymington, New Forest
Hampshire, England

TWO DAYS LATER – LATE AFTERNOON

Aurelie Lemieux shooed her niece and nephew before her up the curving cobbled incline as the cottage with its cornflower-blue shutters came into view.

"*Move along, enfants. We are almost there.*"

"I'm not an infant, Aunt Aurelie." Wise beyond her years, Nathalie grinned, her brandy-colored eyes sparkling with pride. "I'll be twelve in three months."

"Indeed, you will," Aurelie agreed.

They were growing up so fast.

A glance at the sun poised in the azure sky dotted with fluffy clouds confirmed the hour was long past two—probably closer to four, in truth.

When one didn't own a watch, one learned to rely upon the sun's placement in the sky to determine the approximate time. Often difficult to do with England's notorious clouds obscuring the golden orb.

Time had escaped them today, which she hoped meant the children had truly begun to heal from their trauma. The loss of their father and home when they were so young was bound to leave scars.

Rémi and Nathalie had become distracted first by the majestic ships anchored in the harbor along Lymington's quay and then by seeking pretty pebbles at Milford on Sea. Aurelie's cloak pockets sagged with the treasures the children had found and insisted on bringing home. The stones would soon grace a special spot in the back garden.

Since she could spare no coin to hire a hackney, they had walked almost three miles to Milford On Sea to explore the enchanting beach. After collecting colorful rocks, shell pieces, and even a prized tern feather, Aurelie and her wards enjoyed a simple picnic of dark bread, cheese, apples, and cold tea.

She'd taken the opportunity to give them a lesson on tides.

Windblown and far less energetic and talkative than they had been this morning, Rémi and Nathalie had trudged ever more slowly toward their new home the last half-mile.

Catching their small hands, Aurelie swung them back and forth, higher and higher in the air.

"Hurry along, *mon chous*. Aunt Marie expected us to return almost two hours ago."

"Aunt Aurelie, you spoke French." Nathalie giggled. "But I do not mind. I like being called a cream puff."

Tugging at their hands, Aurelie gave the children a playful smile.

Their serviceable shoes clicked on the cobblestones as they grudgingly increased their pace.

Aunt Marie Millard likely still dozed in her darkened chamber with that wretchedly spoiled cat sprawled across the bed beside her—no, draped atop her. Antoinette commandeered every human as her throne. *And* as her servant.

Three troublesome times since they'd moved the household to Lymington last week, Antoinette had escaped into the garden—the last time, late at night—only to prance along the wall, refusing to come down until she was good and ready. Naturally, Aunt Marie remained blissfully unaware of her cat's penchant for the garden.

She'd likely swoon at the revelation that her beloved puss had ventured into the *wild*.

Wild, indeed.

Aurelie furrowed her brow and tightened her mouth, but only for an instant, lest the children take note and fret that something was amiss. Something was, but the poppets needn't know. They'd experienced enough hardship and heartache in their short lives.

Aunt Marie wasn't well; her constitution was fragile and increasingly worrisome.

Nevertheless, the stubborn dame—a distant English cousin on *maman*'s side of the family— insisted that all she required to restore her health was rest and Lymington's milder clime. Traveling to a truly warmer climate to recuperate was out of the question. With diligent economizing and thriftiness, funds remained sufficient for necessities—barely. However, their meager budget could not be stretched to accommodate holidays for even one traveler, let alone four. Five, if one included the cat.

If not for their childless grand aunt's generosity and kind heart, Aurelie and the children would've had nowhere to go after her older half-brother, Gaston, had been arrested three years ago.

She would never believe Gaston had conspired against King Louis XVIII.

Never.

Nonetheless, when the Crown sentenced Gaston to death and seized his assets, leaving his children impoverished and homeless, Aurelie had no recourse but to flee France with what they could carry. They could not remain in a country where the poor were labeled *les classes dangereuses* and *les misérables*, and Gaston's undeserved and unwarranted infamy made it impossible for Aurelie to find a position of employment.

She'd sold every piece of her mother's jewelry for the journey to England except for a sapphire brooch passed down to the daughters in her family for five generations. Aurelie feared that circumstances might necessitate the pawning of that precious memento too.

If only she could find a paying position.

What good would that do?

Pursing her lips, she shook her head but quickly stilled the movement before the children could ask why.

Between caring for her failing aunt and the energetic children, tending the cottage, and cooking, Aurelie had scant time for a job. Not to mention that she also acted as her niece and nephew's tutor. The single servant who accompanied them to Lymington spent most of her time running to and fro for Aunt Marie rather than cooking and cleaning as she had originally been hired to do.

A wind gust flicked Aurelie's bonnet ribbons across her cheek, and a black-headed gull screeched overhead.

In truth, she wasn't certain how much longer finances would allow them to keep Tabitha Palgrave on. The decision to move to Lymington was as much about Aunt

Marie's health as it was a fiscal necessity. Though Aunt Marie was entitled to live at Strathem-Whiteley until her death, they simply could not afford to keep the large house in Cheshire open any longer.

A restrictive clause by a long-ago relative prevented selling Strathem-Whiteley, so the servants had been let go, the furniture covered, the windows shuttered, and the doors locked. It stood empty and tomb-like waiting for another male Millard to inherit the estate.

Mayhap Aurelie could give French lessons, though not all English welcomed the French despite the war between their countries ending a decade ago.

She cast a skeptical glance over the neat cottages.

Would anyone in this sleepy township want to learn French?

Not likely, which put her back at square one.

"I'm hungry, Tante Aurelie." Rémi glanced up, his dark brown eyes hopeful yet shadowed with uncertainty. Small for his ten years, he had experienced deprivation.

They all had.

How Aurelie despised the circumstances that had forced them into this untenable situation.

"Remember to speak in English, Rémi. It's aunt, not *tante*." She softened the reprimand with a smile as she swiped a lock of thick sable hair off his forehead. "We'll have a nice cup of tea and ginger biscuits in the garden."

And chicken soup with brown bread for dinner. Again.

"Sing with me." Aurelie gave a playful little skip.

It would keep the children's minds off their tiredness and hunger, and it was also how she helped them improve their English. They'd sing a verse in French and then in English.

"*Sur le pont d'Avignon,*" Aurelie sang.

Rémi and Nathalie did not join in.

"Children." She gave them a mock frown. "Let's start again, shall we?"

"*Oui,*" they agreed in unison, somewhat less than enthusiastically.

> "*Sur le pont d'Avignon*
> "*L'on y danse, l'on y danse,*
> "*Sur le pont d'Avignon,*
> "*L'on y danse tous en rond.*"

"Now in English, please." Aurelie squeezed their little hands—such fragile little hands.

> "*On the bridge of Avignon,*
> "*We dance there, we dance there,*
> "*On the bridge of Avignon,*
> "*We dance there in circles.*"

"See, we are home already." She nodded toward the neat row of houses along the curved lane, each small front courtyard encased by a low brick or rock wall.

The poppy-red door to the cottage beside Candle Glow Cottage opened, and a finely dressed, broad-shouldered gentleman stepped over the threshold, silver-topped walking cane in hand. Unlike most other cottages, his bore no sign or plaque proclaiming the dwelling's name.

He was breathtakingly handsome, and her feminine interest stirred for the first time in a very long while.

Could he be the man from the garden?

Aurelie slowly took in his masculine form.

From his long legs encased in shiny Hessians to his form-fitting black trousers displaying well-muscled thighs to his emerald-green and gold paisley waistcoat and forest-green jacket edged in black velvet spanning admirably wide shoulders, he bespoke quality and wealth.

His eyes met Aurelie's across the cobbled track, and the most inexplicable jolt zipped outward from her chest, spreading to her arms and legs. For an instant, she wished she wore one of the elegant and costly walking ensembles she'd left behind in France rather than a sensible, unremarkable slate-blue gown and cloak.

Oh, yes. The pink silk—an exquisite gown in Aurelie's favorite color.

Non. Non.

She swiftly corrected her wayward musings.

She'd left that life behind.

No, she'd fled that life to save hers, and her brother's children.

Aurelie must accept her fate...her lot in life...whatever had brought about this reduction in her circumstances. No matter how unfair or disheartening. Doldrums and melancholy weren't in her nature. In point of fact, she was annoyingly optimistic most of the time.

Hadn't she been told that too many times to count?

"Can we go inside?" Rémi tugged on her hand. *"S'il vous plait?*

"*Oui.* Go along with you. Wash up for tea, please."

His boyish grin told her he'd caught her slip into French too.

Trying not to appear too forward, Aurelie eyed the gentleman from beneath her lashes, using her bonnet's brim to afford her a bit of surreptitiousness.

Was he the man she'd spoken to two nights ago?

The one who'd helped get Antoinette off the brick wall?

The man with the most mesmerizing baritone Aurelie had ever heard?

His attention shifted to her niece and nephew before veering to her face once more.

Were his eyes brown?

The brim of his beaver top hat cast a shadow over his

upper face, making it difficult to determine the exact shade.

Rémi trotted forward and opened the unoiled wrought iron gate. Its seldom used hinges creaked in protest, and Aurelie made a mental note to oil them. A moment later, he disappeared into the cottage, his sister hurrying behind his small form—the gate wide open behind her.

Aurelie must remind them to close doors and gates lest Antoinette run away. Such a loss would crush Aunt Marie, who doted on the feline like a child.

Aurelie returned her attention to the imposing man.

Perhaps he was as uncertain of her identity as she was his.

One hand on the gate, she canted her head.

"Bonjour."

Never before had she greeted a gentleman she hadn't been introduced to, but something about this man had captivated her the other night. Silly and foolish, of course. Regardless, there was nothing wrong with being friendly to a neighbor. Surely greeting him in French would alert him that she was indeed the woman he'd spoken to the other night.

Seabirds called in the distance, but he remained silent.

Humiliatingly and aggravatingly so.

When he didn't return her greeting, a flush crawled from Aurelie's chest to her hairline, leaving a scorching path in its wake and heating her face. No doubt her cheeks glowed like hot coals.

With a casual nod, the gentleman continued on his way, dismissing her as easily as one did a servant pouring tea or sweeping the street. Perhaps he was a snob or a social climber. What was the English term? A mushroom?

Mushroom?

That made no sense, but then much about the English baffled her.

Or... *Zut*, why had Aurelie not considered this before?

The gentleman might very well be married.

That would explain his reserve.

Profound and illogical disappointment swept through her, and she shivered when another burst of mild seaborne wind buffeted her. With a sigh, half-regret and half-weariness, she made her way into Aunt Marie's cottage, taking care to secure the gate behind her.

Dinner would not prepare itself.

Before closing the door, Aurelie couldn't help but steal one more glance at the mysterious gentleman as he strolled along the sloping lane toward the seaport.

At one time, she'd dreamed of marriage. A family. Children.

Destiny had denied her those, but she had Gaston's children to raise.

It would be enough.

It must be.

THREE

Another superb brandy
Lymington

29 APRIL 1826 ~ ANOTHER SPLENDID SPRING MIDNIGHT

As he had most nights since arriving in Lymington a fortnight ago, Adolphus enjoyed a glass of spirits while staring at the stars. Only here did he feel truly relaxed, unencumbered by the weight of responsibilities. That itself proved irrational because he still had duties—scores of them.

Wasn't he in Lymington to oversee his investments? Which, by the by, were coming along splendidly. The nearly finished schooner was nothing short of magnificent. Too bad he'd never stand atop her deck as she dipped and peaked on ocean waves.

He would name her, though he had not yet settled on an appropriate name.

Grazing a finger along his jaw, he stretched his legs before him.

Mayhap this contentment wasn't as much about a reprieve from obligations but the lack of artifice and toadying directed his way. He could get accustomed—very accustomed—to this serene life, though he knew these interludes were just that: a brief, tranquil escape from a very comfortable and most privileged prison.

He understood why the cat next door had braved the outdoors and refused to respond to her mistress's fervent pleas to come inside. Her pretty mistress had kept him awake two nights contemplating what she looked like, where she was from, what her name was, only to have those musings crushed under the weight of reality.

She had children. Which likely meant she had a husband.

C'est la vie.

He understood the spoiled cat. Like him, she relished her freedom, no matter how temporary or fleeting, and no matter how luxurious her jail.

"Meow. Mrrrow."

As if coordinated by fate, the object of his thoughts announced her presence with a throaty purr. One of the objects of his thoughts, that was. The other he'd tried unsuccessfully to banish.

Adolphus swung his attention to the wall as a whiff of honeysuckle wafted past again.

"Good evening, your majesty." He lifted his half-full cut crystal glass. "Are you supposed to be outside?"

Would the delectable Frenchwoman next door put in another appearance?

His pulse leaped at the thought.

He slid his focus to the small ladder he'd placed beside the house in case the inquisitive cat returned. Yes, it was where he'd left it.

Stretching, Antoinette chirped flirtatiously. "*Me—ow.*"

"I'd bet my best bourbon, you naughty minx, that your pretty mistress has no idea you have given her the slip again."

His profound reaction to the lovely blonde who lived at Candle Glow Cottage had left him bewildered and wary. Unlike many of his peers, he didn't engage in flirtations with married women—particularly women with children.

That he hadn't considered his neighbor wasn't available pricked his conscience and pride.

One thing was for absolute certain. Adolphus was *not* in Lymington to engage in a flirtation, so it was just as well that the lovely temptress was unavailable.

Though why he continued to think of her in those terms did not bode well and deserved further contemplation.

This afternoon, her wholesome beauty had rooted him to the pavement and left him tongue-tied—both completely foreign reactions to attractive women.

Antoinette stretched her length along the wall, utterly at ease and uncaring that she intruded upon his solitude.

Flick. Flick. Swish.

She moved the tip of her tail up and down.

Up and down.

Peeved or flirting?

"*Meow.*"

"If you think I'm getting up and petting you, you had better think again."

Adolphus was far too relaxed, content, and reluctant to move from his comfortable spot.

But what if her mistress wasn't aware the precocious creature had ventured outdoors?

It was none of his concern.

He looked overhead, deliberately pointing his focus elsewhere.

By God, he wasn't playing nursemaid to a bloody cat.

"*Meow. Meow.*"

He took a sip of the umber liquid before quirking an eyebrow upward.

Demanding creature, wasn't she?

A tiny, almost ignorable prick of guilt twisted his stomach.

What if the cat belonged to the children?

The prick grew into a gnarled wad.

No child should lose their pet.

At the tender age of ten, Adolphus had lost his favorite foxhound. Atlas had escaped the stables again. The dog loved nothing better than to run in the fields and meadows, chasing rabbits, foxes, and squirrels. He'd not returned in the evening as was his wont. A stable hand had found Atlas's body two days later on Westbrook land bordering the Hartigans' property.

The beloved pet had been shot and left to die.

Just another reason the Westbrooks held no affection for the Hartigans. Though Old Man Hartigan claimed an overzealous steward had shot Atlas because he feared the dog would chase their cattle, Adolphus had always wondered if that were true or if one of Hartigan's sons had been the culprit.

Dragging his morose thoughts back to the present, Adolphus skimmed the wall.

The cat had disappeared.

Tensing, he levered upright.

Where was she?

Momentary panic for an animal that wasn't even his seized him.

Ah, there she was.

He let out a long breath.

The ornery cat had meandered to the far end, where she stared at the cobbled lane below.

Swish, swish, swish went her tail.

"Don't you dare," Adolphus muttered in annoyance as he swiftly set aside his glass and angled to his feet. "I am not chasing you all over Lymington in my stockinged feet."

It took but a trice to retrieve the ladder, place it against the wall, and collect the cat, who didn't seem to mind that a complete stranger held her.

She gazed up at him with half-closed, insipid blue eyes and dared to purr. Loudly.

"Antoinette?"

A woman holding a small oil lamp emerged from the shadows near the back of the cottage.

Ah, the mysterious Frenchwoman and—*lucky me*—delectable in her nightclothes too.

Not an unwelcome surprise at all.

Adolphus rested a forearm on the bricks, stroking the cat with his other hand. Wicked cad that he was, he leisurely looked his fill. Her white gown and robe, along with her unplaited halo of golden hair hanging around her shoulders and down her back, gave his lovely neighbor an ethereal, almost angelic appearance.

"Antoinette?" She slowly turned in a circle affording

him a view of her nicely shaped bottom. "Kitty, kitty. Are you out here?"

"Indeed, she is."

"Oh!" A harsh exhalation met his pronouncement before the neighbor lifted the lamp higher and spotted him lounging against the top of the wall with her cat in his arms.

"It's you," she gasped.

Who had she expected?

He peered beyond her to the doorway cast in wavering shadows from the crabapple tree. No light illuminated the opening or the windows. The rest of the household must be fast asleep.

Including her husband?

That notion cooled Adolphus's ungentlemanly musings swifter than a midnight dunk in yon harbor ever could have done.

Regardless, he couldn't suppress a grin at her obvious discomfiture.

She was quite adorably flummoxed. To her credit, she recovered with admirable swiftness and aplomb. Head angled, she smiled, and the radiance of that simple upward sweep of her mouth lit the garden as if the moon had drifted to earth for a sacred, soul-penetrating moment.

Now it was his turn to be discomposed and confounded.

Waxing bloody poetic too.

What was it about this midnight nymph that beguiled him?

Adolphus slid a hand over the cat's soft, white coat.

"She looked as if she considered jumping onto the lane, and I thought I better apprehend her before she did so that you would not have to hunt for her through the streets at this hour."

"I must thank you for rescuing Antoinette once more, *monsieur*. One of the children must've left the door cracked again. I shall remind them to be more careful."

"I suppose I should introduce myself, as this is becoming a habit." Adolphus dipped his chin in what would have to suffice as a bow as he still balanced on the ladder. "Adol..."

God's teeth.

Like a besotted young buck, he'd nearly blurted the truth and given himself away.

Get a grip, old chap.

He cleared his throat.

"That is, I am Ab Westbrook."

"Aurelie Lemieux," she answered without hesitation.

Miss? Missus? Lady?

She placed the lamp on a small, lopsided round table before dragging a chair to the wall below him. With child-like adroitness, she nimbly hopped onto the seat and lifted her hands for the cat.

"Antoinette is my aunt's cossetted pet. Aunt Marie

would have an apoplexy if she knew the cat had escaped the house. She worries Antoinette will get lost. Candle Glow Cottage is hers."

"Ah, I thought perhaps Antoinette belonged to one of your children."

Tucking the naughty puss beneath one arm, Aurelie curved her pretty mouth into a rueful half-smile. "*Non.* The children prefer dogs, but Aunt Marie fears a dog would scare Antoinette. I don't believe anything would scare her, and a puppy might help my niece and nephew heal."

Niece and nephew?

Well, now...

Interest, potent and compelling, surged through Adolphus's blood before he firmly squelched it. He wasn't about to ruin his cherished oasis with a romantic interlude. Even if a siren as enticing as Aphrodite stood mere feet away.

She'd said her niece and nephew needed to heal.

From what?

The loss of their parents?

Something else too?

Did she also have wounds?

Aurelie climbed down from the chair but continued to gaze up at him.

What color were her eyes?

In the half-light, Adolphus couldn't tell, but a thick

fringe of sooty lashes framed the large, round, and slightly inquisitive orbs.

Somewhere in New Forest, a tawny owl hooted, reminding him he stood in his stockings atop a ladder, chatting with a woman in her nightclothes. In the distance, a dog barked a warning, and a seaborne breeze teased her curls.

"I shall bid you goodnight, Miss Lemieux."

When she didn't correct his form of address, rather primitive masculine possessiveness slammed into Adolphus with such force that, had he been on the ground, it would've rocked him back onto his heels. Instead, he nearly toppled backward off the ladder onto his arse.

He gripped the wall to steady himself, hoping she hadn't noticed.

She hadn't.

She rubbed her cheek against the cat's fur. That innocent, but to his heightened senses erotic, act had him digging his fingertips into the rough bricks.

He welcomed the pain.

It centered him and brought him back to his senses.

Devil take it! Adolphus Benedict Haygarth Westbrook. Stop this addlepated balderdash.

"*Bonne nuit,* Monsieur Westbrook." She half-turned and then glanced over her shoulder, a hint of bravado as well as shy uncertainty in her stance. "Would you like to come for tea tomorrow?"

Would he?

Did whales swim?

Did hawks fly?

Did the sun rise every morning?

Was he the future Duke of Latham?

"Of course, your wife is most welcome too," she said a trifle too nonchalantly.

Sly minx.

He hid a pleased grin.

Was that her way of asking without coming right out and asking if he was married?

Did that mean Adolphus had piqued her interest too?

"I'm not married."

Her eyes widened the merest bit, but the insufficient light prevented him from detecting joy or gladness in her gaze.

He shouldn't accept her invitation. It might complicate things enormously. Probably would, in truth.

Yes, Adolphus would refuse.

That was the prudent thing to do.

He didn't particularly want a cozy relationship with his Lymington neighbors. If things went sour, it was far worse than if they'd never become acquainted. How well he'd learned that very thing from the Westbrooks' bothersome relationship with Hefferwickshire House's closest neighbors—the Hartigans.

However, his confounded tongue refused to obey his mind's logic, and instead of declining her invitation, he blurted, "What time?"

"Half past three." Then she disappeared into the house before he could refuse.

Adolphus wasn't certain how long he stood on the ladder staring at the door she'd disappeared through. Only when his toes began to ache from gripping the round rail did he come back to his senses.

"I'm in trouble," he mumbled as he descended the ladder. "Bloody, big trouble."

FOUR

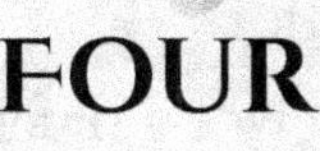

Candle Glow Cottage's Parlor

THE NEXT AFTERNOON ~ FIVE AND TWENTY MINUTES PAST THREE O'CLOCK

Aurelie rearranged the tea service and cups on the tray for the third time. They weren't fancy china or expensive silver, but the charming Spode Blue Italian service would still suit. Across the parlor with its sun-bleached floral damask draperies and furniture, Rémi and Nathalie lay on their stomachs on an equally faded but clean Aubusson carpet and played a game of checkers.

Aurelie had the distinct impression Candle Glow Cottage had not seen human occupancy in at least a decade. Likely much longer. Still, the house boasted a provincial charm and simplicity that was quite appealing despite its lack of splendor.

A glance at the rosewood bracket clock atop the unlit walnut hearth revealed five minutes to half past three.

Would Mr. Westbrook come?

He hadn't exactly agreed that he would but had only inquired what time tea was. Not that Aurelie had given him a chance to decline. That was awfully bad of her, but the truth was, she wanted him to agree.

It hadn't taken much cajoling to get Aunt Marie into the parlor during her usual naptime, especially with the promise of Maid of Honor tarts, Shrewsbury biscuits, and—most thrilling of all—a *male* guest. Despite the temperate weather, a hand-knitted, lilac-colored throw covered her arthritic knees as she sat like a queen holding court in the room's lone overstuffed armchair.

"Westbrook, you said?" Hard of hearing, Aunt Marie fairly trumpeted the question, her voice echoing loudly in the parlor.

Both children shot her startled glances before returning their attention to their chess game.

They'd grown quite fond of their distant relation despite her unconventional ways.

"Yes, Aunt. Ab Westbrook." This was at least the fifth time Aurelie had repeated herself. Auntie seemed quite fascinated with the name, though she said she couldn't quite recall why.

"Hmm." Aunt Marie drummed her gnarled fingertips on the chair's worn arm. "Westbrook. Wonder if he's any relation to the Duke of Latham Westbrooks?" she pondered more to herself than Aurelie.

"I win." Nathalie's victorious cry interrupted Aunt Marie's oral musings.

Rémi scowled before giving a good-natured grin. "Let's play again."

They swiftly picked up their respective black and red pieces, and the game soon engrossed them once more.

As if she hadn't heard Rémi or Nathalie, Aunt Marie narrowed her eyes in deep contemplation.

"If I recall, there are scads of them. Six brothers, each with at least five offspring. And that's not including the late duke's brothers and their hoards." She dimpled and gave a mischievous wink. "A fruitful lot, those Westbrooks and their brides."

"I'm sure I wouldn't know, Aunt Marie. We didn't discuss Mr. Westbrook's family."

In truth, Mr. Ab Westbrook and Aurelie hadn't discussed much but the bothersome cat.

"I danced with a Westbrook at a soirée when I first came out. Cannot remember if it was Solomon or Benedict Westbrook though." She shook her head, causing the lace-edged cap atop her head to slide forward. "Several decades do tend to blur one's memory. A handsome chap with nice eyes, as I recall. Naturally, I hadn't met my Milford yet. Once I had, I had no eyes for any other man. I even turned down an offer from a viscount to marry him."

She chuckled, her focus far away in another time and place.

"Oh, the tongues that wagged. How could I choose a commoner, even if he was landed gentry, over a noble?" A melancholic smile arched her mouth. "Love. The choice was easy."

Aurelie had never met Uncle Milford, but Aunt kept a small portrait of the plain man with kind eyes on her nightstand.

She had stretched the truth a wee bit to explain their expected guest for tea, for Aurelie couldn't very well reveal she'd extended the impulsive invitation at midnight while donned in her night attire. All while retrieving Antoinette from the garden again.

Aunt Marie might suffer an apoplexy.

No, Aurelie merely said she'd met their neighbor and invited him to tea in an attempt to be cordial. She had met him on the lane. Aunt needn't know he hadn't spoken to her.

After all, this was their new home. It couldn't hurt to become acquainted.

Aunt Marie smoothed a hand over Antoinette's shiny coat.

"Bet he's one of the distant relations. Would explain why he lives here." Her expression took on a calculating aura. "Is he handsome? What does he do for a living? Is he married?"

"No, Aunt. He is not."

"He's not handsome, or he's not married?" Aunt Marie asked with feigned innocence.

Aurelie recognized what her wily aunt was up to. Her attempts at matchmaking these past three years had grown ever more bold and daring. And humiliating.

The haberdasher. The neighbor's bachelor son who always smelled of fish. The widowed vicar. Aunt Marie's solicitor's brother—who'd been fifty if he'd been a day.

If Aurelie married well, all their circumstances would improve. The crux, however, was no one was interested in a dowerless French emigrant responsible for two children and an aging dame. Although to be fair, Aunt Marie's funds had kept them housed and fed these three years past —much to Aurelie's chagrin and guilt.

A knock echoed on the front door, saving her from having to respond to her aunt's probing.

Aurelie nodded to Tabitha to answer.

Mr. Ab Westbrook—*what an unusual first name. Perhaps short for Abner or Abbot?*—had come after all.

That didn't explain the unexpected giddiness or why Aurelie hurried to check her chignon in the mirror marred by blackish-grey spots above the slightly lopsided rose-wood half-table near the doorway.

A few seconds later, Tabitha returned.

Alone.

Four pairs of eyes bored into her.

"That was Mr. Westbrook's man of service." She bobbed her head as she went to straighten Aunt Marie's lap blanket. "Mr. Westbrook sends his apologies. There was an incident at the docks involving one of his ships."

"*Ship-sss*?" Aunt Marie emphasized the plural 's' and looked like a cat with a bowl of fresh cream. "How unfortunate. We shall, quite naturally, extend another invite."

Of course, they would. Especially since Auntie now knew Mr. Westbrook had a connection to ships, albeit his involvement might be as minor as drawing the plans or recommending sailcloth.

Aurelie motioned to the children.

"Come, Rémi. Nathalie. Let's try these Maid of Honor tarts, shall we? I used raspberry jam instead of cheese curds and sprinkled them with sliced roasted almonds."

A rare treat, indeed.

Rémi and Nathalie scrambled to their feet and then hurried to sit side-by-side on the settee, where they waited with admiral patience for Aurelie to pour their tea. Whereas most adults preferred children not be present for tea or meals, she believed it could only benefit them to practice their manners.

Not that they had much chance to do so.

Stratham-Whiteley House had been quite isolated, their nearest neighbors almost a mile away.

Still, that didn't mean Aurelie didn't serve tea daily with at least one baked dainty so that her niece and nephew could rehearse the etiquette lessons they'd learned.

Perhaps it was just as well that Mr. Westbrook hadn't come. He was a distraction Aurelie could ill afford, and entertaining girlish fantasies at four and twenty wouldn't do.

She quickly prepared everyone's tea before adding tea to the dab of milk in her cup and dropping in a sugar lump. Once everyone had a cup of tea, selected a tasty pastry, and munched happily, Aurelie wandered to the window, teacup in hand.

The sapphire sky blended with the green-blue sea on the horizon. A pair of crows hopped along the cottage's roof across the way, and a half dozen seabirds soared in a circle above the quay.

The tableau ought to have charmed her—might've done another time.

Not today. Not now.

Her disappointment made no sense.

She'd only spoken to Mr. Westbrook three times and

seen him but twice—all brief interludes. Naturally, as a man of commerce, he must attend to his business when the need arose.

That demonstrated he was responsible. Reliable. Steadfast.

Yes, but she'd used a precious allotment of sugar to make the sweets. Oh, Rémi and Nathalie—Aunt Marie and Tabitha too—were in heaven at the extra treats. Normally, Aurelie only baked ginger biscuits or shortbread.

She turned from the window and made her way back to the others.

Just as she sat, someone rapped on the front door again.

"Who could that be?" Aunt Marie asked, selecting another Shrewsbury biscuit.

"Perhaps the milkman. I asked him to leave an extra bottle of milk on his next round."

The children were growing so much that they needed the nourishment.

Tabitha, intent on rearranging Aunt Marie's blanket and helping her adjust her position in the chair, sent Aurelie an inquisitive glance.

Aurelie waved her away. "I'll get it."

Brushing Shrewsbury biscuit crumbs from her second-best gown—a pale blue affair with no adornment save a strip of lace at the collar—she opened the door.

Mr. Westbrook stood there, breathtakingly handsome and windblown. Today, his quality dove-gray tailcoat and cream-toned pantaloons tucked into Wellingtons displayed his masculine physique to perfection.

Her heart took on a new rhythm.

"Mr. Westbrook."

Overcome with rare maladroitness, Aurelie could form no other words.

He appeared adorably boyish and vulnerable but also excitedly virile.

"Am I too late to join you for tea?"

"No, of course not." She stepped aside. "Do come in."

He did so, casually glancing around the spartan entry as he removed his hat and gloves.

"Let me take those for you."

His fingers brushed hers as he passed her his possessions, and that tingle that had thrummed through her the other day sent a frisson throughout her once more.

She automatically glanced upward, and his gaze snared hers.

His tobacco-brown eyes darkened even further.

Good heavens.

She would have to guard her heart well from this charming rogue.

Using the pretense of placing his possessions on the hall table, she summoned her equanimity with an alacrity she hadn't known herself capable of.

"Shall we?" His mouth tipped upward into a rogue's smile, and he extended his elbow.

Aurelie gingerly placed her fingertips atop his rock-solid forearm as she guided him to the parlor. As they entered, the room went utterly still, every eye trained upon them.

Tabitha wasn't present.

She must've taken the opportunity to tend to a few household chores.

"Mr. Westbrook was able to join us for tea after all," Aurelie offered needlessly.

He broke into a self-confident smile.

"I apologize for my tardiness. One of my shipbuilders took a nasty fall, and I wanted to ensure he received immediate medical care."

His shipbuilder?

Aunt Marie caught Aurelie's eye, a decidedly I-am-well-pleased speculative glint in the elderly woman's pale blue gaze. The precocious dear probably already mentally constructed a wedding guest list.

"That was very judicious of you, Mr. Westbrook." Aunt Marie offered her hand as if she were a grand duchess. "I've looked forward to making your acquaintance."

He dutifully bent over her fingers. "And I yours."

The sly bounder sent Antoinette, curled contentedly in Aunt Marie's lap, an innocent glance. As if he'd never seen the wretched creature before, and yet Aurelie couldn't scold him for keeping secret the naughty cat's midnight ventures.

"That's a lovely cat," he said with another roguish smile.

With those four words, he utterly won over Aunt Marie.

"Antoinette. My pride and joy." She beamed. "Aurelie, introductions, please."

Aurelie made the introductions.

Rémi executed a perfect bow and Nathalie an elegant curtsy.

Aurelie couldn't prevent the proud smile curving her mouth.

"I am very pleased to make your acquaintance," Mr. Westbrook said, taking a seat on the remaining settee.

"Do you know why our cottage is named Candle Glow Cottage, Mr. Westbrook?" Nathalie asked in excellent English.

"I do not." He tilted his head and smiled. "I should like to know."

"It's because a sea captain used to own this cottage." She swung her legs back and forth as she talked. "When he was away at sea, his wife kept a candle lit in the window until he was home safe again." She sighed. "Isn't that romantic?"

"A charming story, indeed," Mr. Westbrook agreed.

"Why doesn't your cottage have a name, Mr. Westbrook?" Rémi helped himself to another Shrewsbury biscuit.

Excellent.

The lad needed to put on a bit of weight.

"I don't know, in truth." Mr. Westbrook didn't appear as if he much cared whether his cottage bore a quaint title.

"You should pick a name." Nathalie looked at her brother. "We could help you."

They'd come up with something silly such as Crumpet and Curds Cottage.

"Whether Mr. Westbrook wants to name his cottage is his business, children." Aurelie offered an apologetic smile.

He answered with a sensual upward sweep of his mouth, sending her pulse cavorting like newborn lambs. "I shall consider it. Why don't you make a list of potential names for me to consider?"

Excited smiles wreathed Rémi and Nathalie's faces, and a tiny piece of Aurelie's heart plopped at Ab Westbrook's feet.

Stroking Antoinette, Aunt Marie said, "Tell me, Mr. Westbrook. Are you related to the Duke of Latham Westbrooks?"

FIVE

*FIVE EXCEEDINGLY LONG TICK-TOCKS OF THE
MANTEL CLOCK LATER*

Bother and blast. Bollocks too.

And there it was.

Adolphus barely restrained a groan and an eye roll at Mrs. Millard's obvious fishing expedition. He'd not missed her keen, speaking glance toward Aurelie at his arrival. The aunt displayed all the telltale signs of a matchmaking huntress, and if there was one thing Adolphus couldn't abide, it was being stalked.

Particularly under false pretenses.

Had the invitation to tea truly been a spur-of-the-moment gesture or a cleverly seized opportunity?

He supposed it was expected that someone would recognize the Westbrook name. After all, his was a large and extended family.

As he took a sip of rather decent tea, he wrestled with telling his hosts who he truly was or weaving another thread into the lie of omission Adolphus had begun when he'd purchased the cottage next door.

"I am indeed a relation." Adolphus bit into a Maid of Honor tart and nearly groaned as delicious flavor burst in his mouth. His cook didn't bake such delectable confections. "This is delicious. I adore anything with almonds."

Most nuts, truth to tell.

Many evenings, he sat before the hearth with a brass nutcracker and cracked nuts for an after-supper snack.

"Aunt Aurelie made them." Holding a tart herself, Nathalie gave a little bounce on the settee, causing her dark curls to pirouette. "Her almond biscuits are wonderful too. She's a *really* good cook. And she's smart. She taught Rémi and me English. Plus, she's very pretty."

Her French accent thickened with her increased excitement.

And the impish darling had successfully alleviated the need for him to expound on just precisely how he was related to Latham.

Nathalie smiled sweetly before flicking an almond off her tart and into her mouth with her tongue.

Nevertheless, Adolphus had the distinct impression she was up to matchmaking shenanigans too. Although Nathalie was right—her aunt *was* pretty. Very pretty, truth be told.

Aurelie gave her niece a bewildered glance.

Or was her confusion an act?

A ploy to appear innocent in what was becoming increasingly apparent as a calculated scheme?

"You are being impertinent, my dear," Aurelie said in gentle reproof, the merest hint of color skating up her delicate cheekbones. "We do not boast or brag about ourselves or others, particularly in front of guests."

"I don't know what *pertnant* means." Nathalie scrunched her face. "But I was only telling the truth."

Mrs. Millard chuckled and waved rheumy fingers toward the little girl. "The child gets that headstrongness and directness from my side of the family."

What a surprise.

"It means impolite," Aurelie said gently, delightfully fetching in her simple blue gown. The shade flattered her gray eyes and made her hair appear all the paler, as if moonlight had been spun in the soft strands. "And it makes our guest uncomfortable."

Adolphus admired the firm yet kind manner in which Aurelie reprimanded the child. Motherhood came naturally to her, even though these children weren't hers by birth. What circumstances had compelled her to take on the responsibility?

He suspected the tale wasn't pretty and the circumstances most dire.

Nathalie's lower lip trembled, and she cast her gaze to the floor.

Pity for the child stirred in him.

"We have a few headstrong, independent females in my family too," Adolphus said, setting his teacup down. "In fact, my sister is a better shot with a pistol than most men. And my grandmother...Well, I have never known another woman as determined and obstinate as she."

Rémi crammed what was left of his tart into his mouth, chewing happily as he glanced between his sister and Mr. Westbrook.

He winked. "Both women are utterly delightful, precocious, and intelligent too."

That did the trick.

Nathalie perked up. "They are?"

"Indeed," he assured her. "Few can match their wit."

Grandmama was a spirited old bird, and Althelia had blossomed into a confident young woman. Such was not always the case, and that blame could be laid at the Hartigans' feet.

Adolphus glanced over to find Rémi staring at him

now with a solemness better suited to a man of the cloth or a barrister.

"Do you have a wife, Mr. Westbrook?"

Another confoundingly direct Lemieux, it would seem.

"Rémi!" Aurelie gaped at her nephew, the color draining from her face before bright red streaks skated up her cheekbones. She shook her head. "Why would you ask such a forward thing?"

"Because you need a husband," the lad said matter-of-factly and then, with a shrug, stuffed half a Shrewsbury biscuit in his mouth. "Papa said so many times."

"It's true." Nathalie nodded. "You do."

Adolphus choked on his tart, and Aurelie gave him three rapid slaps on his back.

Husband?

He'd been right.

This invitation was nothing more than a brazen attempt to find Aurelie Lemieux a husband.

The winsome Miss Lemieux was on the matrimonial prowl and had decided to sink her claws into him—after only three brief encounters.

Did that make her desperate or just brazen?

"Please accept my apologies, Mr. Westbrook." Chagrin and a hint of vexation tinged Aurelie's pretty gray eyes, the color of the ocean after a storm. "I have no idea why the children have taken it upon themselves to be so impudent."

Or so she claimed.

Quite convincingly too.

Nevertheless, Adolphus didn't believe a word of it.

He'd been pursued since before he came of age—had nearly been trapped in a compromising situation with a woman ten years his senior who coveted a title more than her virtue or reputation. Thank goodness, Father had caught wind of the scheme and put a swift and permanent end to Muriel Wheatman's wiles. The last he heard, she had married a decrepit old sot three times her age. She had her title though.

Perhaps steering wide of this opportunistic family was prudent as well. Apparently, they had an agenda, and Adolphus wanted no part of a marital trap. Odd that he should experience such regret about not furthering his acquaintance with his intriguing midnight visitor.

Normally, women didn't get beyond his carefully guarded parapets. That Aurelie Lemieux had managed to so swiftly ought to have alerted him.

"Rémi, Nathalie, please apologize to Mr. Westbrook and then go to your rooms." Aurelie turned her attention on each of them in turn, and the children fairly squirmed in penitence. "I shall speak with you later."

Rémi rubbed the toe of his shoe across the worn carpet. "Apologies, sir. I meant no offense."

His genuine remorse touched Adolphus. How could he blame the children for doing what the women had told them to do? Perhaps even coached them. He'd wager he wasn't their first victim either.

"None taken." Adolphus extended his hand.

His brown eyes rounding in surprise, the little chap grinned and clasped Adolphus's palm.

"Nathalie?" Aurelie coaxed, her tone firm but not stern.

"I apologize too, Mr. Westbrook." She bit her lower lip, blinking away tears. "Does this mean you'll never come to tea again? We have so few guests..."

"That is not of import right now." Aurelie put a hand on each of their shoulders and turned them toward the doorway. "Please go to your rooms. I'd like an explanation when I speak to you about your untenable behavior."

Stilted silence descended upon the parlor as the children clasped hands and departed with their heads lowered.

Inhaling a deep breath, Aurelie faced him. Hands entwined before her, she offered a fragile smile.

"Nothing the least awkward about that," she quipped. "Please permit me to extend my apologies again as well. It seems a lesson in what constitutes polite conversation is in order."

"Oh, pshaw." Mrs. Millard waved her plump hand. "The darlings meant no harm, as I'm sure Mr. Westbrook is aware."

Actually, Adolphus wasn't.

Was it possible the two imps had come up with the peculiar remarks of their own accord?

Yes, but as likely as the British abandoning tea as their favorite beverage.

"They love you and want you happy, Aurelie. That is all." Mrs. Millard ran her fingers through Antoinette's fur. "They know what you've sacrificed. For them. For me. This was their way of trying to compensate—to make it up to you in the only way they know how."

Just what had Aurelie Lemieux sacrificed?

Why was the family here and not in France?

One thing was for certain. Adolphus was not telling them who he was. Not yet, in any event. If they had set their sights on him as husband material before they knew he was a marquess and future duke, who knew what they were capable of?

He stood. "I thank you for the tea."

"I hope you'll come again," Mrs. Millard said as the cat hopped down. "Lymington is to be our home now, and we know no one here save you."

That was not his concern.

Adolphus refused to feel guilty that he had no intention of furthering their acquaintance.

Antoinette pranced to him and wound her way between his boots, purring loudly.

"She likes you." Approval reverberated in the matron's

tone. "That's a good sign. Animals are very intuitive about humans' characters."

"I shall see you out, Mr. Westbrook." Aurelie half-turned toward the door.

"No need." He softened the refusal with a disarming smile. The polite one he used to erect a barrier but also appear genial. "I know the way."

"Very well." Something flashed in her eyes. Hurt? Dismay? Understanding? She knew he was giving them the brush off. "Thank you for being our guest this afternoon."

She'd retreated behind icy politeness too.

As he closed the door to Candle Glow Cottage and strode the few feet to his doorway, Adolphus couldn't shake the niggling feeling he'd made a major mistake.

He glanced toward the cottage he'd just left, half expecting to see Aurelie peeking at him from behind a curtain. That's what a huntress would do.

Only she wasn't.

SIX

* * *

High Street Saturday Market – Lymington

6 MAY 1826 ~ SIX DAYS LATER ~ MID-MORNING

Aurelie adjusted the nearly full shopping basket on her arm before picking up and examining a well-made pair of children's leather boots. Rémi had outgrown his shoes and desperately wanted a pair of boots for his birthday next week. She couldn't justify a frivolous gift, but Rémi needed this new footwear, and the cost wasn't too terribly dear.

"A good choice, Madam." The dapper salesman clasped the lapels of his ugly plaid suit and thrust out his lower lip. "Double leather soles will prevent your youngster from wearing a hole in the bottom. Shall I wrap them up for you?" he asked hopefully.

"Yes, please." Nodding, she glanced around. She still hoped to find stinging nettle at the herbalist to make tea to alleviate Aunt Marie's arthritis.

The merchant gathered the footwear and set about wrapping them for her.

Aurelie's heart leaped slightly when she spied Mr. Westbrook across the street at a stall displaying shawls, capes, gloves, and other female accessories. Though he faced partly away from her, she'd recognize his broad shoulders, square jaw, and strong nose anywhere.

She hadn't seen him since his abrupt departure from tea last week, nor had she heard him in his garden. Twice, she'd snuck out near midnight like an errant child, straining her ears to hear the slightest sound from beyond the brick wall.

Only deafening and lonely silence met her intense scrutiny.

The last time, she vowed she wouldn't do so again.

What would she say in any event without Antoinette as an excuse?

Perhaps he'd chosen to refrain from his midnight capers, afraid further contact with her might put him at risk of becoming leg shackled. At first, embarrassment and chagrin regarding her family's impudent insinuations had buffeted Aurelie. However, as the days passed, vexation and resentment raised their repugnant heads.

Mr. Westbrook had no right to treat her dismissively when she hadn't remotely hinted at anything untoward. As if she ever would manipulate a man into marriage or flirt outrageously as the pretty brunette helping Mr. Westbrook did without compunction.

The woman had honed in on Mr. Westbrook like a bee to honey. Her mouth curved into a coy smile, and she gave a coquettish laugh as she placed her palm on his forearm. About as subtle as a pony in petticoats.

He chuckled at something the flirt said before selecting a pair of pink gloves and a breathtaking pink and ivory shawl edged with rose-colored fringe. They were beautiful pieces, and a tiny twinge of envy pricked Aurelie. She'd always been drawn to pink, and today was no exception. A woman somewhere was very lucky, indeed.

An unsolicited and unpleasant thought assailed her.

He'd said he wasn't married. He'd never said he wasn't courting anyone, wasn't betrothed, or didn't have a mistress.

Not that he'd likely volunteer the latter.

Look away, Aurelie Dominique Eugenie Lemieux.

Zut. You are not a green schoolgirl.

Mr. Ab Westbrook had made his feelings clear as glass. He wanted no part of her or her family. Yet, Aurelie's confounded eyes refused to obey her stern admonishment.

The woman leaned in, brushing her voluptuous chest against Mr. Westbrook's arm and murmured something in his ear—bold as a dockside *putain*.

Chuckling, he shook his head as he passed her a few coins.

Curving her mouth into a practiced *moue*, the merchant folded the shawl before wrapping it and the gloves in tissue paper.

"Ah, Widow Kushman has set her sights on our Mr. Westbrook, it seems."

The shoemaker's casual comment yanked Aurelie's attention back to his tidy stall.

"You know Mr. Westbrook?" she asked with what she hoped was casual nonchalance.

"Only by reputation." He passed Aurelie the boots wrapped in brown paper and tied with a string. "A man who simultaneously builds three ships and is a major investor in the salterns cannot help but stir interest in our small community."

He was wealthy then.

Strange that he chose to reside in a simple cottage rather than at the hotel or buy a larger house.

She added the boots to her basket, their weight a reminder that Rémi was growing up.

"May I presume you, too, are acquainted with him?" Friendly brown eyes peered at Aurelie.

"Only just. Mr. Westbrook is a neighbor." She smiled

and shifted the weighty basket to her other arm. "Thank you. My nephew will be thrilled with the boots."

"I included my card in the package. If the boots need repairing, I do so free of charge the first year." He puffed out his chest. "I take great pride in my work."

"That is very generous of you." Rémi would likely outgrow the boots before they wore out.

Aurelie turned around and plowed straight into a hard male chest. Strong hands gripped her upper arms, balancing her. Her nostrils twitched at the merest whiff of cloves.

"Careful there," came an amused male voice. "Cannot have a lass as pretty as you falling, now, can we?"

"I beg your pardon, sir."

Retreating a step, she glanced up into the greenest eyes she'd ever seen beneath thick, tawny eyebrows.

A gentleman in his middle thirties grinned down at her, his eyes crinkling at the corners as if he smiled often. He wasn't handsome in the dandified manner of Beau Brummel, but he had pleasant features, and his eyes gleamed in appreciation as he skimmed his gaze over her. His attire bespoke wealth but wasn't pretentious except for a ruby glinting in his ascot's snowy folds.

"No harm done." He swept into a half bow. "Roland Trammel, at your service, miss...?"

His unabashed attempt to learn Aurelie's name should have annoyed her, but it amused her instead.

"Miss Aurelie Lemieux."

"You are new to Lymington, Miss Lemieux?" He tipped his gray felt hat upward on his forehead a couple of inches. "I come from a long line of Trammels who've lived here, so suffice to say, I know just about everyone. We own the Puddle Duck Tavern, the King's Coffee and Chocolate House, and Trammels' Restaurant and Hotel."

Ah, the grand building dominating the town's south entrance.

His mannerism wasn't boastful or arrogant but rather matter-of-fact. As if he was so accustomed to his position and community standing that he thought little of it.

"I moved to Lymington with my aunt, niece, and nephew a short time ago."

Out of the corner of her eye, she saw Mr. Westbrook approaching, his purchases tucked beneath his arm. Time to make a hasty retreat.

"Please excuse me, Mr. Trammel. I must finish my shopping and return home. My outing has already taken me longer than expected."

"Of course." He flashed another disarming smile as he pulled a card from his pocket and passed it to her. "I would be honored if you would bring your family to the coffee and chocolate house and enjoy a beverage on me."

She glanced at the card. "I'm not sure..."

Would it be unseemly?

Would accepting his kind offer cause unwanted speculation?

Aunt Marie and the children would adore the treat.

"If I am not there, just present my card, and you shall have your pick of the menu."

He glanced over her head, and his features sharpened minutely. So subtly, in fact, that she would not have noticed had Aurelie not been studying his face and trying to ascertain his motives.

"Ah, Westbrook." Mr. Trammel dipped his chin in greeting. "We've another newcomer to our little corner of heaven. Miss Lemieux, may I introduce Ab Westbrook?"

Aurelie painted a serene expression on her face and forced herself to meet Mr. Westbrook's eyes. A flintiness she'd never seen there before hardened the corners of his face.

"We've met, Trammel." He glanced at her laden basket. "In truth, we are neighbors. We share a brick wall in back and a stone fence in front between our properties."

"Neighbors, you say?" Eyebrows drawn together, Mr. Trammel looked back and forth between them.

"Indeed. Let me take that for you." Before Aurelie could object, Ab slid the basket off her arm and onto his. He placed his tidy package, neatly tied with a lavender ribbon, on the top.

"I am quite capable of carrying my shopping basket, Mr. Westbrook."

"I have no doubt, but what kind of gentleman would I be if I didn't assist you, particularly since we are walking in the same direction?"

Rather than make a public scene and argue that she wasn't going home just yet, Aurelie bit her tongue. That didn't mean she wouldn't give the overbearing brute a tongue-lashing the moment they were alone.

"It was nice to make your acquaintance, Mr. Trammel." She made a point of glancing at his card again before tucking it into her reticule. "I shall speak with my aunt, and perhaps we shall accept your generous offer."

"I hope you do." He nodded, his gaze boring into hers with such potent intenseness, she averted her eyes. "Excuse me, please. I see someone I need a word with."

He darted into the crowd and soon disappeared.

The stinging nettles would have to wait until another day.

Aurelie turned toward the cottage, refusing to let Mr. Westbrook see that he had her at sixes and sevens. The arrogant bounder. Taking her basket and implying he had the right to escort her home.

She walked with him for several feet, waiting until most of the crowd was behind them.

"That was over-bold of you, Mr. Westbrook. I am four and twenty, not a young miss who requires a chaperone, nor are we such intimate acquaintances that you can speak on my behalf. I was not finished shopping."

He remained silent for several paces.

"Forgive me for overstepping, Aurelie, but I don't believe you are aware of Trammel's reputation as you are new to Lymington. He's a charming philanderer you'd be wise to steer clear of."

"I did not give you leave to address me by my given name, Mr. Westbrook."

Why must she go all prickly on him?

She sounded like a prude.

He was only being helpful.

Wasn't he?

"It's a very pretty name." He winked, and she missed a step.

Charming devil.

"Can I tell you a secret, Aurelie? First, you must promise to tell no one."

Aurelie should say no.

She shouldn't encourage whatever this was. The man blew hot then cold from minute to minute. How was she to maintain her composure with his vacillations?

"Is it something improper? Illegal? Inappropriate?"

She'd not promise not to tell if it was.

"No." He crossed his free arm over his chest. "I swear upon my family name."

"Very well." She nodded as they began the gentle

incline to Harbor View Lane. Though she couldn't imagine why he wanted to reveal a secret to her when he'd left tea so quickly last week that he'd fairly left a cloud of dust in his wake. One would have thought the household was riddled with the plague.

"My given name is Adolphus." At her startled glance, he added, "I abbreviated my first and middle names for anonymity."

She pursed her lips and cast him a speculative glance.

"Why would you wish to remain anonymous?"

"*That*, my dear Miss Lemieux, is a secret I am unwilling to share."

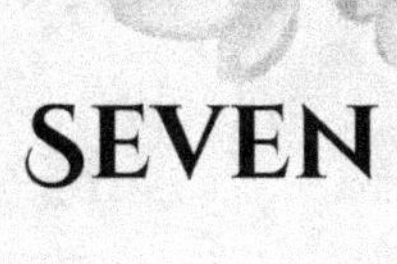

SEVEN

STILL ON THE WAY HOME

Adolphus shouldn't have told Aurelie his name. If she didn't keep her word and shared that information with her meddling aunt, his identity might be revealed to all of Lymington. Yet he'd wanted to make amends for his abrupt departure from tea and his interference at the market, though the latter was for her benefit and the former for his.

The prudent thing to do would be to continue avoiding Aurelie Lemieux but, confound him for a fool, the woman fascinated him. From that very first night when her sultry laughter had filtered over the garden fence, there'd been a powerful connection between them.

She felt it too.

It made no sense. It wasn't logical, but Adolphus couldn't explain the potent feeling away.

He'd seen her furtive glances when she thought he wasn't looking. Had noticed Aurelie's breath quickening, her lovely gray eyes—the color of London fog in January—flexing the merest bit at the corners, and her petal pink mouth slightly parting.

Oh, yes.

She'd sensed this unnameable thing—this scintillating undercurrent.

The aunt had as well, and possibly the children.

Perhaps that is why they'd all hinted—broad as a hippopotamus's hind end—about Aurelie's unmarried status.

His as well.

"I shall keep your secret, Mr. Westbrook."

Their heels clacked on the time-worn cobblestones as they ascended the hill. "I cannot presume to know your reasons, but I hardly think something as insignificant as a name would cause a great dust-up."

For the average person, probably not.

For a future duke, assuredly so.

"Thank you. I appreciate your discretion."

They'd reached the top of the road and turned toward their cottages on Harbor View Lane, his to the left of hers.

She put her hand out for the basket.

Adolphus lifted his package from the top and passed it

to her. He twisted his mouth into a grin. "For my sister's birthday. She quite adores pink."

"It's my favorite color too." A becoming blush tinted Aurelie's cheekbones at the unexpected admission.

Adolphus tucked that detail into the back of his mind. One never knew when a tidbit such as that might be useful.

"I think you and my sister would have a lot in common. Althelia would rather receive a gift from a small market than one of Bond Street's elite boutiques." He grinned. "She's unusual in that way and many others as well."

"She sounds like a remarkable young woman." With a nod, Aurelie turned toward her cottage. "Good day, Mr. Westbrook."

"Miss Lemieux?"'

She pivoted back toward him. "*Oui.* Yes?"

"Tell the children I would welcome their suggestions for a name for my cottage."

Why had Adolphus said that?

He was in no hurry to plaster some absurd moniker on a sign.

Crested Tit Bottom or Hideaway Haven.

God save him.

He bloody well knew why he'd done it, to have an excuse to see her again.

Even when he knew the prudent thing to do was to cease interacting with these neighbors.

She raised a skeptical winged eyebrow—mistrust, caution, and confusion narrowing her gaze. In the afternoon sunlight, her eyes rivaled the ocean's mystical gray after a storm.

"*Non*. I'm not certain that is wise. Rémi and Nathalie can be..." Aurelie half-grimaced. "*Creative* and not always in a fitting manner."

A reluctant grin skewed his mouth upward on one side. Part of him would like nothing better than a shocking and wholly unsuitable name nailed to his front door.

Well, perhaps not.

He remembered quite well the nickname his siblings called him. *Fussy Fuss*.

Zounds, to this day, it set his teeth on edge.

Adolphus wasn't fussy.

Just particular. Less so in Lymington than in London, which begged the question. Why?

"Only appropriate names will be considered." He shifted his sister's gifts to beneath an elbow. "If I like a suggestion, I'll have a sign maker in town create a placard to hang on the cottage door."

A genuine smile blossomed across Aurelie's face, wreathing her features in delicate beauty.

Breathe, you dolt.

That such a simple act could render him mute and addlepated should have sent him trotting into his house, slamming the door and locking it behind him. Instead, he stood there like a besotted swain, waiting for her reply.

"I shall tell them. It is most kind of you, Mr. Westbrook." She entered the small enclosed yard, then glanced toward him as he opened his gate. "Shall I have their suggestions delivered to you?"

She was reluctant or afraid to extend him another invitation.

Just as well.

Whatever maggot had prompted him to make the ludicrous offer he would no doubt come to regret had been silenced by the devil on his shoulder whispering caution in his ear.

He couldn't be too vigilant.

"That is acceptable." He sounded stilted and formal to his ears.

He loathed the formal stuffiness that had become his marquess persona yet didn't know how to cast off that shroud and just be Adolphus.

"I'm leaving the day after tomorrow." He jostled the package. "Attending my sister's birthday celebration."

Glancing down, Aurelie put a gloved finger to the package topping her basket. "Rémi's birthday is next week too. He wanted new boots."

The disparity didn't escape Adolphus.

He'd bought Althelia frivolous accessories. Aurelie had purchased a necessity.

Her dark-lashed eyes searched his as if she tried to understand his motives. Her expression cleared, and with another nod, she slipped into Candle Glow Cottage.

The day after tomorrow, he was off to Hefferwickshire House for Althelia's birthday. A fortnight spent away from Lymington ought to cool any future speculation anyone entertained about a match between him and the enchanting Miss Lemieux.

Would that it cooled his libido and his growing interest in the captivating mademoiselle.

EIGHT

The Cottage Garden

Aurelie trailed her fingers through the lone birdbath in the charmingly unkempt garden. Slowly, the overgrown beds and shrubberies were taking shape. She had no experience with gardening and little time to spare tending the small yard, but she found puttering about the plants satisfying. She'd hired a local adolescent to help with the heavier tasks until she had restored the garden.

She'd lain atop her mattress for two hours, tossing and turning, throwing her covers off, then yanking them back on again. Finally, the unseasonably warm night stirred her from her bed and drew her outdoors.

Bare toes sinking into the cool grass, she slowly wandered the enclosure.

Why couldn't she stop thinking about Adolphus Westbrook?

What cause had he to be secretive about his real name?

At tea the other day, he'd admitted to being a relation to the Duke of Latham Westbrooks but had not clarified the connection. Perhaps he was a close relative and didn't want the attention such information would garner.

Aurelie couldn't blame him.

In any event, continuing to dwell on the enigmatic man was fruitless and pointless.

Nevertheless, her thoughts wandered to him over and over again.

Attired only in her night rail—who would see her?—a sigh slipped past her parted lips as she glanced overhead. A few wispy clouds here and there obscured stars, but most of the sky twinkled with diamond-like stars dotting the inky blackness.

She glanced at the wall separating the garden from Adolphus's.

Was he out there again?

It seemed to be a habit of his to spend the evening outdoors.

How little she knew of the man and that she wanted to know more perplexed her.

She'd had her share of handsome, charming beaus in France—had even been betrothed at nineteen. But Janvier had died, and though she'd mourned his passing, she'd not been heartbroken.

Her parents' marriage had been a marriage of convenience. A widower, Papa already had a son, but his bankrupt estate needed funds. Mama, an heiress with a slight limp and thoroughly on the shelf at six and thirty, accepted the only marriage offer she'd ever likely receive.

Desperation proved quite a motivator.

Her parents had been content, if not precisely happy, and Aurelie held no illusions that *Père* had been faithful to *Maman*.

The same was true of Gaston.

His marriage to a plump, dowdy heiress with no prospects had also been arranged. How unfair that an unattractive, penniless man—if he had a title or a prestigious name—could marry well, but a destitute woman without beauty couldn't hope to make a match.

She placed a palm on the coarse wall, almost as if willing Adolphus to be on the other side...and to somehow know she was there.

Waiting for him.

Fool. Fool.

Silence reigned except for a lone cricket's melancholic music and the persistent waves caressing the shore.

With another wistful sigh, she turned away from the wall, accidentally bumping into a metal watering can in the muted light. It clanked as it toppled over, the clatter unnaturally loud in the stillness.

"Aurelie?"

Adolphus *was* there.

She stepped nearer to the wall.

"Adolphus?"

How odd that with these bricks between them, they needn't worry about convention and could simply be a man and a woman. No need for formality and conventions.

"I wasn't sure if you were there." She bit her lower lip in vexation when the confession made her sound rather desperate, as if she prowled about in the middle of the night, hoping to talk to him.

There were names for women like that, and none were complimentary.

But wasn't that exactly what she'd done?

No. Not intentionally.

Are you sure?

Zut. Hush.

She gave her conscience a mental scolding.

Something other than cool evening air had drawn her outdoors.

Aurelie didn't have the words for this enigmatic beckoning—this indefinable allure.

The magnetism had been there since that first night and only seemed to increase in intensity with each encounter. These emotions were absurd, yet she was powerless to stop whatever this was. In truth, though it would certainly lead to heartache and perhaps heartbreak, she was powerless to resist.

Could Adolphus feel the same?

A provocative look in his eyes when they were together suggested he might want to, but something held him in check.

"I usually enjoy a brandy and the stars before retiring while I am in Lymington," he said. "I cannot do so in London."

She digested that revelation for a moment. "So Lymington is not your home?"

"No."

He offered no more information, and Aurelie would bite off her tongue before prying.

"Why are you out here at this hour?" Though his tone was conversational, a seductive timbre infiltrated his voice, sending a shiver scuttling up her spine. "I didn't see Antoinette."

"No, thank goodness. She is fast asleep on top of Aunt Marie's bed."

The cat could not be blamed for this midnight excursion.

"The children have been better about keeping the garden door closed." They did try to be well-behaved, but they were children, after all. "I couldn't sleep. I was too warm and came outdoors to cool off."

"May I ask you something personal, Aurelie?"

He'd drawn nearer. It sounded as if he stood next to the wall as Aurelie did—only a few inches separating them. It might as well be an unbreachable chasm.

"You can ask, but I cannot promise to answer."

Life had taught her caution and wariness. Trust could not, and should not, be easily given. The unscrupulous held no compunction about using trust against a person.

He chuckled, the melodic tone resonating in the still night air.

"Why is it I expected you to say that, Aurelie?"

She smiled to herself.

Adolphus had begun to know her, and that knowledge shouldn't please her as much as it did. It was dangerous and futile to let her heart yearn for something that could never be.

"What happened to cause you and your niece and nephew to leave France?"

She leaned her forehead against the cold, hard, unforgiving bricks, reliving the anguish and heartache.

"My half-brother was accused of treason and executed." Pain sluiced her, cramping her lungs and squeezing her heart. Even after three years, the grief hadn't completely subsided. "The charges were fabricated. I believe the king wanted to seize his land and wealth."

"It would not be the first time a king of France did so," Adolphus remarked, compassion in his voice. "So you fled?"

"Yes." She nodded, though he couldn't see her, and swallowed the familiar lump tightening her throat. "Else the children would've been tossed onto the street." Her too, and Aurelie had no wish to become a *putain*. "Trust me when I tell you that life is worse than death. If not for Aunt Marie's kind heart and generosity, our fate wouldn't have been much different in England."

"Lymington is to be your permanent home?" he asked.

Somewhere in the forest paralleling the shore town, an owl hooted.

"It is." What else could she say?

We are not paupers, but neither are we flush in the pocket.

Small town life is far more economical than a country estate or living in a city.

My lot in life is to care for an elderly woman in failing health and to raise two children and pray they can make their way in a harsh, unforgiving world.

"I should like to live here myself." Wistfulness

threaded his tone, and she thought she also detected notes of hopelessness and futility.

Aurelie tilted her head.

Why don't you make this your home? Wait and see if this unacknowledged, unnamed thing between them would grow—flourish?

Instead, she softly asked, "Why don't you?"

Silence descended and lengthened into uncomfortable tension. Even the happy cricket ceased chirping. The very air seemed to still in anticipation of his answer.

Was that too forward of her?

How was her personal question any different than his?

Seconds ticked on with no response.

Was he still there?

"Adolphus?"

"I'm here."

Yes, distinct despondency and reluctance weighted his words.

"Forgive me. It is none of my business." It wasn't, though Aurelie wished it could be. "I didn't mean to pry."

Yes, she had, even if it was imprudent and impolite. She was curious to learn everything she could about this fascinating man. Even if it wasn't wise and could lead nowhere.

"You didn't. No more than I did with my question about why you left France." He cleared his throat. "Just as circumstances beyond your control forced you to leave your homeland and care for your brother's children, there are factors that dictate my choices and future."

"I see." She didn't really. But she wouldn't poke her nose further into his business. "But if you were free to do as you wish, what would that be?"

His deep chuckle resonated in the stillness. "That's easy. I'd travel the world. Sail to every place I've ever wanted to visit on one of my ships. Perhaps even captain the ship myself. *If* wishes were horses..."

"Beggars would ride," she finished.

"What about you, Aurelie? You must've had dreams before you fled France."

She'd had splendid dreams, but those cherished yearnings were lost to her now.

"Aurelie?" That melodic timbre would tempt a nun to shed her habit and dive into the ocean naked. "I shared my dreams. Won't you trust me with yours?"

She laid her palm against the brick. "Mine weren't so adventurous or daring as yours. I wanted to marry for love, have several children, live in a quaint old house with several dogs, and grow roses."

Silence met her confession. It settled upon the night like a shroud.

She gave a self-conscious laugh. "I told you they weren't impressive."

"I think..." Adolphus cleared his throat. "I think they are splendid. Truly splendid."

Tears sprang to her eyes—because of his kind words and because of hopes lost.

"I should retire." Aunt Marie would question the dark purplish half-moon shadows beneath her eyes from lack of sleep again.

"I think I'll stay out here a while longer. I relish the solace and peace late night affords me."

An epiphany struck.

His life wasn't his own.

He didn't want people to know who he was.

Adolphus Westbrook was the Duke of Latham's son.

Aurelie knew at once that she'd inadvertently stumbled upon the truth.

Which son, though?

Aunt Marie said his grace had seven sons—two adopted.

A little sleuthing would no doubt reveal the truth. But did Aurelie have the right to uncover the secret when Adolphus had taken such care to remain anonymous?

Before she could muzzle the words, they slipped off her tongue.

"Because your other life—that is your ah, position—doesn't allow you those luxuries?"

His low, sensual chuckle raised fresh goose flesh along her arms. Lord, her reaction to this man was at once alarming and tantalizing.

"You are very astute, Aurelie."

Too blasted astute.

She'd preferred not to have known. Because if Adolphus was truly the duke's son, he was too far above her for there to be anything between them except for this unexpected and likely temporary friendship they'd struck up.

"*Bonne nuit*. Safe travels."

Heart heavier due to the uninvited revelation, she faced the house.

"Aurelie?"

Hopeful, she half-turned in anticipation.

Of what?

"Yes?"

Half a dozen heartbeats passed before he finally murmured, his voice gruff, "Sweet dreams."

Something more than disappointment flooded her.

"*Merci.*"

She'd reached the entrance when he whispered something that sounded very much like, *Dream of me.*

NINE

BREAKFAST THE NEXT MORNING

Unshaved, hair uncombed, and dressed only in a shirt and pantaloons, Adolphus buttered a piece of toast as he ruminated about the unexpected encounter in the garden last night. The encounter that had kept him awake, staring blankly at the ceiling, until dawn this morning. And which left him looking like he hadn't tended to his grooming or slept in a week.

Aurelie's hopes and dreams had been crushed under the responsibilities thrust upon her. She'd accepted her fate, not bemoaning her present life. *How unfair*, something inside him raged.

As much for her forfeited dreams as for his own.

He'd risen—more aptly, dragged his doleful arse from

bed—determined to resume his persona as a respectable peer of the realm. He'd even progressed as far as fastening his cuff links and draping a pristine cravat around his neck before, with an oath that would make his outrageous Grandmama blush, he yanked the neckcloth off and tossed it on the bed.

Why must Aurelie continually beleaguer his thoughts?

Pulling his eyebrows into a tight vee, he swore beneath his breath.

"Bollocks."

Hell and damnation too.

He'd unintentionally said too much—revealed too much to her.

And her keen wit had not only seized upon what he *had* said but, even more disturbingly, on what he had *not* said too.

A ping on his plate alerted him that he hadn't secured his right cufflink engraved with the Edenhaven crest—a knight's helmet and sword. The silver rectangle glinted next to his sausage and eggs.

Once he'd resecured the cufflink, he returned to his torturous contemplations as he smeared marmalade on his toast.

Just how much had Aurelie figured out?

Did she suspect the truth?

What if she did?

In point of fact, Adolphus had half expected someone

in Lymington to recognize him before this, which was one reason he eschewed the local gatherings and ignored the invitations that periodically came his way.

He wasn't in Lymington for entertainment or socializing.

Though not nearly as popular as Bath or Bristol, a few members of the *haut ton* ventured to the coastal township on occasion. That was the other reason he had kept to himself.

He didn't need a busybody blathering all over London and beyond that the Marquess of Edenhaven had a secret lair in Lymington.

His brothers would like nothing more than to descend upon his sanctuary. They'd always considered him sanctimonious, and they were right. He hadn't the freedom to be himself as they had.

When had he become distrustful?

So cynical?

It wasn't any way to live.

Adolphus had already decided to distance himself from his tantalizing neighbor. His mind applauded his resolve while his libido and mayhap his heart cursed him for a thousand kinds of fool. He could avoid Aurelie, but he was as reluctant as Hades to give up this cottage—his little piece of heaven.

Yet, if Aurelie began snooping around...

Perhaps he'd forego his garden routine tonight. It was

but one night, after all. Besides, he left for Hefferwickshire before dawn tomorrow. After last night's sleeplessness, a good night's slumber was in order.

His conscience spared him no mercy.

That's a poltroon's excuse.

Yes. Yes, it was.

Because although Adolphus resolved otherwise, he would likely spend another fitful night musing over Aurelie's creamy skin, mesmerizing light gray eyes, provocative curves, and witty intellect.

You're a bloody fool, Adolphus Benedict Haygarth Westbrook.

An unseen force compelled him to lift his attention and gaze out the open door to the garden.

What the devil?

He froze, scarcely believing his eyes, and then a heart-beat later, jumped to his feet with such force that his chair toppled backward and the butter knife clattered onto his plate before landing on the table.

Arms spread wide, Rémi balanced atop the wall, gingerly making his way toward Antoinette, who was splayed at the other end and watching his progress with unqualified arrogant feline disparity.

"Here, kitty. Come here, Antoinette."

Face pale and pinched, the boy took another wobbly step forward.

"Antoinette," he pleaded. "I don't want to get in trouble. Aunt Aurelie told me to be more careful with the door. Must you always be so naughty?"

Fear shook Rémi's voice and his small body as he valiantly crept toward the disdainful cat.

How in thunder had the lad managed to get on top of the wall in the first place?

The crabapple tree?

Adolphus shifted his attention toward the lone tree tall enough to allow the child access.

Rémi tottered, leaning to the side on one leg but managed to right himself.

Adolphus's breath hitched in his lungs before leaving in a painful-relieved whoosh.

How in all of perdition did the boy think he would get down while holding the cat?

Having once been a lad, he doubted the child had thought that far ahead.

Lest he startle the boy and Rémi lose his balance and fall, Adolphus stifled another oath as he rushed toward the doorway.

The ladder.

He veered a brief glance to where it lay propped against the cottage's side.

Should he get the ladder?

Did he have time?

As Rémi neared Antoinette, the ornery little beast stood, flicked her tail, and then hopped down.

Before Adolphus could decide about the ladder, Aurelie's distraught cry filled the morning air.

"Rémi! What are you doing up there?"

Fear riddled her voice, causing it to pitch high on the last syllable and sending a finch to wing.

The boy shot an alarmed glance over his shoulder, the movement causing him to misstep.

Hell's clanging bells.

Adolphus sprinted across the grass, yet his gut shouted even as he lengthened his stride. He wouldn't get to the boy in time to catch him.

Rémi hit the ground with a hollow thud, his shrill howl of pain turning Adolphus's blood to ice.

"Rémi!" Aurelie shrieked. "Oh, God. Ré-mi!"

"I'm here, Aurelie," Adolphus said to calm her as he knelt beside the sobbing child.

"Where does it hurt, lad?"

"Is he all right?" Panic rendered her voice husky. "Is he hurt?" A heartbeat later, she muttered in disgust, *"Zut.* Naturally, he is hurt, bird wit. Else why would he have cried out?" she scolded herself.

Despite the seriousness of the situation, a reluctant grin twitched the corners of Adolphus's mouth.

"Adolphus. Please say something!"

"I'm not sure what his injuries are, Aurelie."

Adolphus touched the child, now curled into a fetal position and clutching his lower left leg.

"Give me a moment to examine the boy."

"My ankle." Tearfully, Rémi raised huge, agony filled eyes to his. "It hurts."

"I'm sure it does," Adolphus soothed, eyeing the appendage that had already begun to swell.

Broken or sprained?

"Should I send Mason for the physician, sir?" Worry etching her plump face, Tildy, his maid, hovered inside the doorway. She twisted her hands in her apron.

"Yes." Adolphus gave a terse nod. "Have him meet us at Candle Glow Cottage."

Nodding, she trotted to the house's interior, calling for the man of all work.

"Rémi, I'm going to lift you and carry you home. Loop your arms around my neck when I pick you up. Can you do that for me?"

The boy gave a solemn but trusting nod.

"Yes, Mr. Westbrook."

"I shall try not to jostle your leg overly much." Adolphus scooped the child into his arms.

Rémi grimaced as fresh tears leaked from his eyes, but the stoic little soldier clenched his jaw and remained silent.

"Aurelie. I am bringing the boy over. I've sent for the physician. Make ready a place for him, please."

"Of course." A moment later, her garden screen door banged shut. "Tabitha…"

The rest of her words became indistinguishable as she traveled further into the cottage's interior.

Adolphus wasn't such a cynic that he believed Rémi scaled the wall and accidentally injured himself in another attempt to matchmake between Adolphus and the boy's pretty aunt. The problem was that Adolphus could no longer discern what was calculated and what was coincidental, leading him to regard everyone and every situation with acute skepticism.

He didn't much like himself for his pessimism either.

And here he was, having just decided again *not* to interact any further with Aurelie, and Fate—blast her fickle, feckless, manipulating heart—had given him no choice.

TEN

Candle Glow Cottage's Parlor

AN HOUR LATER

Something pulled at Adolphus's heartstrings—something that might've been envy, or yearning, or both—as, arms folded and leaning against the doorframe, he observed the tender family tableau across the room.

Holding her brother's hand, Nathalie hung over the back of the settee. Perched on the seat's edge, Aurelie brushed a shock of hair off the boy's forehead as Mrs. Millard leaned forward in her chair and patted his other hand.

Eyes closed and curled into a contented ball,

Antoinette slept soundly at Rémi's feet. The cat had profound nerve after she'd caused the accident. No one seemed inclined to mention that fact to the cat.

Embarrassed by the attention, the boy, nevertheless, endured his female relations' concern with admirable good grace and humor.

According to Doctor Bresingham, who'd departed a few minutes ago, Rémi's sprain would keep the contrite lad off his feet for a couple of weeks. Thankfully, he'd suffered no broken bones.

Everyone had breathed a sigh of relief at that welcome news.

Adolphus discretely made arrangements to have the physician's bill sent to him as well as any charges for follow-up visits.

Anyone with an iota of perceptiveness could see the family had no funds to spare, yet Adolphus knew beyond a doubt that Aurelie would not ask for or accept charity. He still hadn't decided how to broach the subject of his overreach, which he would eventually have to do. Sooner rather than later, truth be told. But he didn't relish the tongue-lashing he suspected might follow his confession.

A wry grin tugged his mouth upward a fraction.

Now he was a coward too?

Afraid to tell a wisp of female that he'd taken it upon himself to aid her?

No, he feared that proud, independent woman's perception of his actions.

Would she take his help as condescension?

From beneath half-closed eyes, he regarded his new neighbors.

Their love and intimacy tugged at an undefinable emotion and brought an unfamiliar lump to his throat. This was what he wanted in a family—this caring and closeness. Unlike many peerage families, his was loving and supportive. Not only unusual because the aristocracy was notoriously cold, stuffy, and unaffectionate, but simply because of the mere size of his family.

One would think it would have been difficult to maintain close relationships with seven siblings, but despite being a duke and duchess, Father's and Mother's priorities had always been their children, marriage, and family.

A sense of gut-wrenching inadequacy churned in Adolphus's belly.

His parents made it look effortless, but Adolphus didn't believe he possessed their talent or wherewithal to accomplish the same. Unlike Father, Mother, and several siblings, he'd never been adept at expressing his emotions. Besides, though he had a choice of a bride—as long as she was considered *suitable*—the gilded pool from which he could make that selection was profoundly limited.

What were the chances he'd find a wife with the same goals, priorities, and desires as him among the polished, perfumed, and privileged women angling to become his duchess?

He hadn't yet.

None had come within a mile.

His focus lingered on the one woman who *had* piqued his interest.

French. Impoverished. A commoner. Responsible for two orphans and a feeble aunt in her dotage.

And don't forget a fortune hunter.

Hardly duchess material, noted his ducal self with taciturn objectiveness.

How he despised his snobbishness—loathed himself for allowing her circumstances to matter. In truth, Adolphus could overlook all but one—that last and most glaring—of Aurelie's flaws.

Sunlight streamed through the window, casting her in a honeyed glow against the salon's backdrop of faded furnishings. Rather than give the room a tattered and worn-out appearance, it presented comfort and hominess.

He liked that too.

Simplicity over extravagance.

Comfort over luxury.

Unwilling to interrupt them, Adolphus slipped from the room, feeling oddly empty and dissatisfied. And disgusted with himself in a way he'd never experienced before. He'd reached the entrance and gripped the door handle when Aurelie beckoned him.

"Mr. Westbrook, please wait."

He turned, careful to keep his expression bland.

How could he be giddy with joy and overcome with trepidation at the same time?

Since she'd entered his life and turned it topsy-turvy, he didn't know what to expect, least of all from himself. That unnerved Adolphus, for the rigid structure that had once defined him crumbled more with each passing day—and Aurelie Lemieux was to blame, although she remained unaware of her power.

And it must remain that way.

There was no room in Adolphus's life for uncertainty, hesitation, or ambiguity.

Yet an indisputable truth buffeted him. Either by intention or happenstance, this wood sprite had managed to wedge herself beneath his skin, bore deeply into his innermost being, and captivate him.

He could not shake off his fulminating interest, which bordered on obsession.

The feeling was a first for Adolphus. Had he not become leery of Aurelie's intentions, he might've been able to analyze the sentiment and perhaps even act upon the emotion. The war waging within him and the suspicious, accusing devil on his shoulder made him cock a sardonic eyebrow at her.

"Did you need something, Miss Lemieux?"

He didn't trust himself to say her given name.

Doing so caressed his tongue, causing him to speculate what it would be like to whisper it when she lay beneath him. Or when he brought her to completion.

The thought caused an instant and undesired physical response.

Slightly out of breath from rushing to catch him, Aurelie gifted him a brilliant smile.

The impact bludgeoned him.

God save him.

Cheeks adorably flushed and eyes shining, she laid her hand on Adolphus's forearm.

A sensual jolt streaked straight to his nether regions, nearly sending him crashing to his knees.

Sweet Jesus.

More planned seduction on her part?

Adolphus wasn't having it. He wouldn't be teased and toyed with. Seduced by captivating gray eyes and flaxen curls. Lush lips that begged to be kissed and an even lusher feminine figure that beckoned for his touch.

By God, he was the Marquess of Edenhaven, the future Duke of Latham.

Jaw clenched, he fisted his hands.

He'd almost taken the bait but wasn't hooked yet.

Only telling himself Aurelie was an opportunistic, fortune-hunting temptress kept Adolphus from scooping her into his embrace and tasting those sweet, parted lips. Part of him was past caring what her motives were and would gladly heave good sense to the wind, but the pragmatic future duke part demanded he stay vigilant.

Guarded. Impervious.

That part was nigh on to losing this fulminating internal battle. He must put an end to the torture, before he did something rash. Imprudent. Reckless.

For once in his life, do what he *yearned* to do rather than what he was obligated to do.

Bloody, bloody hell.

"I wanted to thank you for helping Rémi. Had you not been home, I don't know how we would've managed."

She seemed so genuine Adolphus almost believed her. God, how he wanted to believe her but didn't dare. Instead, he withdrew his arm and deliberately raised his brows in a superior, condescending manner, certain to raise her hackles.

"I suggest you keep a keener eye on your charges and ensure that such an incident does not occur again. That includes that pesky cat's nocturnal prowls. I value my privacy, and the interruptions have become commonplace."

Shock and chagrin widened Aurelie's eyes, and her pink-petaled mouth rounded into an "O" as she stumbled backward a step. She couldn't have looked more appalled, confused, or hurt if he'd slapped her. She blinked, then blinked again before squaring her delicate shoulders and notching that delightfully stubborn chin upward a notch.

"Of course. I assure you, it shan't happen again." Then seemingly as an afterthought and with a challenge in her flashing gray eyes, she sneered, "*My lord.*"

Every muscle in Adolphus went rigid, and he narrowed his eyes, trying to pry behind her prickly façade.

My lord?

Had she addressed him thusly because she knew who he was or because he acted like an arrogant arse?

What did it matter?

Her affront acted as an additional buffer, and both their defenses and battlements must be fully armed to withstand this mutual attraction. Should their armaments fail simultaneously...

It didn't bear contemplation.

The consequences would prove disastrous.

"See that it doesn't." Expression implacable, he used his most pompous tone. His *I'm an utter blue-blooded assling* tone.

Anger snapped in her eyes, but her furious, unflinching gaze held his.

Lord above, Aurelie's beauty when she was outraged could blind an angel, and he was a mere mortal.

Adolphus opened the door and forced himself to step across the threshold, agonizing over his cruelty in not only eviscerating her but him as well.

Not even waiting until he'd turned away, Aurelie shoved the door shut with such force that the panel hit his rear, the air whooshed past him, and the portentous bang shook the frame.

A pair of matrons gossiping across the low stone walls separating their cottages farther along Harbor View Lane eyed him curiously as he opened the gate and tromped back to his cottage. Only then did he recall his untucked and partially unbuttoned shirt.

By Jupiter, at least his sleeves were properly cuffed.

He glanced downward, and a feral snarl curled his lips.

The right cuff gaped open. The cufflink must've come off when he lifted Rémi.

Bloody perfect.

He looked as if he'd tossed his shirt on after a thorough romp.

Their silvery heads bobbed together, and he hadn't a doubt their speculation would soon buzz about the neighborhood. Well-accustomed to gossip and rumormongering, he didn't miss a step.

Let them blather.

He knew there was no truth to their conjectures.

But what about Aurelie's reputation?

He snorted.

Anyone who believed he engaged in a morning tumble with her aunt and the children present was addled. And if she caught wind of the lurid tattle, she'd be all the more disposed to avoid him.

At least Adolphus had distanced himself from his luscious neighbor once and for all.

It was for the best, of course.

Lymington was his refuge. Soon enough, he'd have to select his duchess, but until then, he'd savor every second of freedom and contentment in this oasis. Once he wed, he doubted he'd ever return to the nameless cottage.

With every step he took, his conscience railed at him.

You've made the worst mistake of your life, you addlepated beef-wit.

ELEVEN

SIX DAYS LATER ~ LATE AFTERNOON

One foot hooked on the coral's lowest rail and his elbows resting on the topmost rung, Adolphus idly observed four of his horses stabled at Hefferwickshire. A brisk wind nipped at his ears as the stable hands exercised the magnificent creatures. Rather than open the house and hire additional servants to oversee the animals at his estate, Hawkshead Court in Sussex, he housed them at the ducal country seat.

God knew Hefferwickshire's stable had plenty of room. Leaving his horseflesh here also saved him time since he didn't have to visit two estates. There was something to be said about the convenience of riding his horses while visiting his parents too.

A horse neighed, and another whinnied and stomped. A cow mooed in an adjacent field, calling for her calf. A calf lowed in response.

"There you are."

Leonidas.

Adolphus glanced over his shoulder to see Leonidas, Fletcher, and Lucius approaching.

Fletcher had spent more time at Hefferwickshire in the past few months than he had in the previous ten years. And he was extremely closed-mouth about why he remained away from London, his gaming halls, and his theater.

"We've been looking for you. Grandmama requests your presence for tea."

"Is it that late already?" Adolphus had lost track of time. Not because watching his horses occupied him, but because he'd been daydreaming about Lymington and a certain pretty neighbor.

"It is." Grinning, Lucius cocked an eyebrow. "And the old girl generally gets what she wants."

That was true.

"Just look what she did last December to get all of us here for Christmastide." Fletcher grunted as he shooed a fly away from his face. "I still haven't completely forgiven her. *'Dire circumstances.' 'Grave situation,'* she vowed. All a ruse."

Lucius propped his elbows on the corral and nodded toward the Egyptian Arabian mare. "She's a beauty. I've never seen a coat that shade of gray. It's almost silver, and she looks quite exotic with that black mane and tail."

"The moment I saw her, I knew I had to have her." Adolphus might not be able to travel to Egypt or Arabia, but he could own a horse that reminded him of those places he'd never visit. "I thought Althelia might enjoy riding her, but she prefers her horse."

Would Aurelie like the pretty mare?

Did she even ride?

Likely she did. Her half-brother had been affluent.

Where in thunder had those musings come from? He nearly cursed aloud, but that would alert his brothers, and he wasn't up to an interrogation.

Every time Adolphus ordered his mind to stop thinking about her, an intrusive thought wiggled its way inside his head, distracting him. And quite often, leading him into a fantasy where he allowed himself to explore all the delightful things about Aurelie Lemieux forbidden to him in the real world.

If only he could be sure she wasn't a manipulative, conniving chit. His gut told him she wasn't, but the evidence suggested otherwise.

Another breeze whipped by, stirring up dust and

teasing his hair and his brothers', as well as ruffling the horses' manes.

Fletcher canted his head, scrutinizing Adolphus with his bottle-green eyes so keenly that he could scarcely remain impassive and not squirm like a lad in short pants.

"Hmm." Fletcher made a low sound in his throat that could've been interpreted a dozen different ways.

Except, Adolphus suspected his older half-brother had deduced something was afoot.

Fletcher had always been too deuced perceptive.

Leonidas glanced between them, then at Lucius. "What precisely does 'hmm' mean?"

"Don't ask me." Lucius shrugged. He squinted at Adolphus. "Do you have something you want to share, big brother?"

"When have I ever shared with you?" Adolphus didn't very often. Though he could joke and laugh with his cousins and friends, he'd always felt a bit of an outsider with his brothers and envied their easy camaraderie.

In fairness, that was probably more his fault than theirs.

Adolphus lowered his foot and brushed residue from the fence from his elbows.

Leonidas gestured toward the house. "Shall we."

Adolphus started forward, then stopped in his tracks and swiveled to face his brothers.

"Since when does Grandmama send all three of you to fetch me for tea?"

He speared each one of them with an accusing glare. "What is this really about?"

They exchanged guilty glances.

Adolphus firmed his mouth. "Out with it."

"Our parents are worried about you." Fletcher scraped a hand through his chestnut hair. "You've been uncommonly quiet during your stay and have kept mainly to yourself."

Nodding, Leonidas said, "Half the time, you don't know when someone is speaking to you, and the other half, you only catch a portion of what is said."

Lucius contrived to look innocent, but a devilish glint shone in his dark blue eyes. "You have all the telltale signs of being in love."

What the devil?

Love?

Adolphus most certainly was not in love.

He drew his brows together into a fierce scowl. "Have you been into the brandy?"

"Of course we have, you dolt." Amusement crinkled Fletcher's eyes, and he slapped Adolphus on the shoulder. "Good attempt at deflection, though."

"Indeed," Leonidas agreed. "Fletcher, why don't you and I go on ahead and let the women and Father know that Adolphus and Lucius will be along shortly? Since

Lucius is in the throes of love at present, he might be able to offer our lovesick brother a spot of advice."

"I am not lovesick or in love," Adolphus snapped.

"Smitten?" Lucius offered with a jaunty grin and a nudge to Adolphus's ribs. "Enamored?"

"Besotted?" Leonidas added with a sly smile. "Enraptured? Captivated?"

Knee bent, Adolphus folded his arms.

When his brothers got like this, there was nothing to do but let them continue in their ridiculousness.

Rubbing his chin, his expression scholarly, Fletcher considered Adolphus. A former doctor, he'd undoubtedly have a few preposterous suggestions too.

He didn't fail Adolphus's expectations.

"Dotty? Bewitched? Mesmerized?"

"Are you done being complete imbeciles?" With a disgusted shake of his head, he started toward the house again.

"Hold there, Adolphus." Lucius sent Fletcher and Leonidas a speaking glance. "Go ahead. We'll be along shortly."

After tossing Adolphus another sarcastic grin, Leonidas and Fletcher strode down the pathway, their boots crunching on the gravel.

"Out with it, Adolphus." Lucius didn't mince words. "You've been moping around in a state of the blue devils. I've never seen you like this. What can I do to help?"

Sincerity rang in his brother's voice and creased his face. If he'd mocked or teased, Adolphus would've ignored him, but he'd offered to help. And Adolphus wanted to talk to someone—needed an objective perspective.

Looking over the pastures and meadows, he sighed and plowed his fingers through his hair. "I've met someone."

"And...?"

"It's complicated."

Lucius canted his head. "Because?"

"Oh, hell. You might as well know, but I swear if you breathe a word, Lucius, I shan't forgive you." Perhaps telling him would give Adolphus proper perspective.

"I give my word, though you know the others will hound me to no end." Lucius attempted a beleaguered expression but failed miserably.

"Lucius. I mean it," Adolphus ground out between clenched teeth. "This is important to me."

"Calm down." Lucius extended his hands, palm out. "I give you my word. I shan't say a thing without your approval or permission."

"Not even to Clodovea?" Adolphus warned.

"Not even to her," Lucius promised.

Where to start?

"There's a young French woman." In short order, he shared about his secret hideaway in Lymington, how he'd met Aurelie, the immediate attraction they'd shared, and the obvious matchmaking attempts by her family. "I don't know if I can trust my instincts regarding her."

Shaking his head, Lucius gave a droll chuckle. "Need I remind you how wrong *my* instincts were about Clodovea?"

He'd mistaken a Spanish noblewoman for a notorious spy, abducted her, and held her prisoner. Now they were married.

"Point taken." Adolphus cut his brother a side-eyed glance. "I envy you and our other brothers. You never have to wonder if a woman is interested in you or your title."

Lucius slapped his shoulder.

"Don't be a dunderheaded arse. It won't matter to the right woman. If you are attracted to this young woman, why not let things play out instead of rejecting her outright? You might discover she is exactly what you want and need. 'Tis stupid to act upon assumptions, big brother."

As they walked to the house, Lucius continued gently berating Adolphus for his stupidity. He only half-listened to the brotherly insults as he planned his departure for Lymington and what he'd say to Aurelie.

TWELVE

Candle Glow Cottage

FOUR DAYS LATER ~ 17 MAY MID-MORNING

As Aurelie had a myriad of times—too numerous to count, in truth—she swept Harbor View Lane with her gaze as she tended the small front beds. The back garden now boasted neatly trimmed bushes, weeded beds, and trimmed grass, so she'd turned her attention to the neglected flower beds at the cottage's front.

"Stop it," she groused to herself. "He's not worth it."

Curving her lips upward, she gave a little finger wave to two matrons chatting across their stone fences, as they did most mornings. Their eyebrows and noses shot skyward before they ducked their heads together. That made three times in the past week they'd snubbed her overture at friendliness.

Perhaps they needed time to warm up to newcomers to their community.

Still, their rejection stung.

Again, Aurelie scanned the lane.

Why did she continue to look for the rude beast who had made it painfully clear he wanted nothing to do with her and her family? She wasn't a loyal dog who'd crawl back to its master even after mistreatment.

I'm only looking because I need to return his cufflink.

She'd discovered it under the sofa two days after Rémi's fall. She didn't recognize the crest, but that Adolphus owned cufflinks engraved with a crest answered the question that had plagued her for days.

Adolphus Westbrook was an aristocrat. A lord. A peer of the realm.

It mattered not.

He mightn't even return to Lymington.

Gardening wasn't just an excuse she used in the pitiful hope she might discover if Adolphus had returned to Lymington. She found the activity soothing. Something was calming and healing in working with the earth. The pretty flowers she'd splurged on brightened the cottage, making it feel homier, less stark and needing of renovation.

Swiping a tendril from her cheek that had escaped her chignon beneath her straw bonnet, she eyed the cottage. It needed painting. What had once been cheery blue shutters had faded to a grayish tone, and paint peeled from the cottage's sides in several places. A dirt-covered trowel in one gloved hand, she placed the other hand on her hip and surveyed the neat row of cottages paralleling the cobbled lane.

Most stood proudly, well-tended, their paint fresh and bright.

She shook her head.

Mayhap she could save enough funds to paint next year.

That reminded her.

Doctor Bresingham still hadn't sent a bill for Rémi's accident.

Tomorrow when she went to market, she'd call on the good doctor and settle the account.

After gathering her gardening basket and placing her gloves, clippers, and trowel inside, she allowed herself one last glance down the lane.

How could she miss someone she'd spoken to but a handful of times?

Especially someone who held her in glaring contempt, though she didn't know why. Except that, if he was indeed a peer, Adolphus Westbrook might believe all commoners were beneath his touch and weren't deserving of basic respect.

It seems the inexplicable connection between them had been entirely one-sided.

More fool her.

"Good morning, Aurelie."

With a startled squeak, she spun toward Adolphus's cottage, almost dumping her basket's contents.

His smoky brown eyes alight with humor, and seemingly uncaring that he dirtied his fine burgundy coat, he leaned his elbows on the rock fence dividing their properties.

Her hungry gaze feasted on him like a starving urchin handed a warm meat pie.

His attire suggested he was on his way out.

Why had he paused to speak with her, acting for all the world as if he hadn't been a horrid beast during their last encounter?

She cast a discrete glance down the lane and almost rolled her eyes.

Yes. Of course, the two snoops unabashedly gawked at Aurelie and Adolphus.

To that point, Aurelie kept her voice low and her mien neutral.

"I wasn't aware you'd returned," she managed with far more composure than she felt, then cursed herself for a ninny for saying the obvious. And because it made it sound as if she'd awaited his return. Which, of course, she had, but he didn't need to know that.

In fact, he mustn't ever know. Not after the way they'd last parted.

"Late last night. I have a few things to attend to in town." Adolphus shoved his hat upward off his forehead. "Would you like to accompany me? We can luncheon at Trammel's Restaurant. I hear the chicken Francese is quite exceptional."

Was he...?

Did he just...?

Aware she stared like a child viewing an oddity at Bullock's Museum, Aurelie blurted, "Why?"

What she ought to have done was turn her back and enter the cottage without another word. But more often than not, when it came to Adolphus Westbrook, her logic and reason took to wing and fluttered away like tipsy butterflies, leaving her to gawp at him like a tongue-tied, moon-eyed nincompoop.

Must he be so devastatingly handsome? So masculine? So...virile?

Surely her cheeks turned apple-red at that last naughty thought.

Adolphus's delighted grin widened and hilarity narrowed his eyes.

"*Why*?" he drawled, lengthening the word into multiple syllables. "Why did I arrive late? Why do I have things to attend to? Why did I invite you to join me? Or why is the chicken Francese exceptional?"

Oh, the teasing rotter toyed with her.

Aurelie would deprive him of the satisfaction of seeing her discomposed.

She would!

Taking a deep breath—because quite naturally, she could not act the shrew with prying neighbors watching —Aurelie angled her head.

"Our previous parting was less than amicable, as you well know. I am trying to discern why upon your return to Lymington, you act as if nothing unpleasant passed between us and invite me to accompany you instead."

She shifted the basket to the other arm, grateful she wasn't wearing the shoddy gown she normally gardened in.

Rubbing his nose, he gave her a sheepish grin.

"The same reason I returned four days early. My brother Lucius is to blame."

"Your *brother*? Is to blame?" Arms folded, she raised an eyebrow. "I fail to see the connection. Please do enlighten me."

What could his brother have said to send Adolphus back to Lymington and cause him to treat her with roguish charm?

"I would be happy to share the details over luncheon." Adolphus glanced over her head, a slight frown puckering his forehead for a second before he returned his attention to Aurelie.

Was it her imagination, or were his eyes softer at the corners?

It mattered not, for Aurelie would not dine with Adolphus.

Not today. Not tomorrow. Not any day.

She required stability in her life, as did her family. He blew hot then cold at the merest whim. Twice, he'd left her cottage with a chip on his shoulder, and she had no more notion now than she did then as to why. Such vacillation couldn't be good for his constitution and wasn't helpful to hers either.

What she did know was that her emotions could not take any more of his on again and off again behavior. Perhaps that conduct was acceptable in the elite social circles he traveled, but Aurelie wasn't interested in constantly guessing his state of mind. Always wondering if she said or did something to offend. And she was done trying to figure this complex, secretive man out.

No. Hers and Adolphus's last parting had not been pleasant, but it had helped her to see clearly. Vividly, in point of fact. If naught else, Aurelie learned from her mistakes. In the future, she'd give Mr. Adolphus Westbrook a wide berth.

"Thank you for the invitation, Mr. Westbrook. Nevertheless, I must decline."

Must for her self-preservation and self-respect.

The shock skittering across his face revealed he hadn't expected her to refuse.

So cocksure of himself.

Wasn't that like an entitled aristocrat?

"Might I ask why?"

He studied her with an intensity that caused a shiver to ripple from her waist to her neck.

"You may, but I shall not answer."

She swiveled toward the door, then spun back.

"By the way, I found a cufflink under the sofa that must be yours." The good doctor would hardly own an engraved, silver cufflink, and no other men had been inside the cottage. "I shall have Tabitha deliver it to your cottage now that you are home."

Aurelie certainly wasn't going to go knocking on his door.

Not with the neighbors making no effort to hide their interest in the goings on at sixteen and eighteen Harbor Lane View. Aurelie hadn't returned the cufflink earlier simply because she didn't know how trustworthy his servants were. A trinket of that quality would bring a few coins, and more than one domestic had profited from their employer's misplaced valuables.

He gave a slow, considering nod, his expression growing impossibly more contemplative. "Thank you. I wondered where I had lost it."

Stilted silence ensued.

When he said nothing else, she procured a polite but impersonal smile.

"Good day, Mr. Westbrook."

"Good day, Miss Lemieux."

Adolphus left his yard and stepped onto the cobbled street, pausing to permit an approaching plum and gold-colored barouche drawn by a pair of stunning bays to pass.

Just as Aurelie opened the cottage door, the barouche lurched to a stop. The horses snorted and stomped their feet at the rough treatment.

"Why I can hardly believe my eyes." A pretty brunette vision in lavender and white ruffles and lace beneath a frilly, fringed parasol batted her lush black eyelashes at Adolphus. "Lord Edenhaven, it *is* you."

Lord Edenhaven?

Aurelie had been right. Adolphus was a lord.

The revelation brought her no joy or a sense of victory.

Go inside, she ordered her leaden feet.

This isn't my business.

Her body refused to budge half an inch. If she was this intrigued, despite her self-recrimination, she didn't want to contemplate what the biddies down the lane would make of it. From beneath her bonnet's protective brim, she veered them a glance from the corner of her eye.

Just as she'd suspected.

The tongue-wagging duo made no attempt to hide their blatant eavesdropping.

"Papa, you remember the Marquess of Edenhaven, of course." She sent Adolphus a sultry smile. "We danced together at the Altringhams' ball last Season."

Aurelie bit her lip.

The woman had—what was the English expression?

Ah, yes. Most assuredly set her cap for Adolphus.

Zut. Non. Aurelie was *not* jealous, for pity's sake.

Seated beside the lady, an older gentleman dressed in the first stare of fashion raised his monocle and raked his gaze over Adolphus.

A gull flew overhead, calling to several others gathering atop the church along with a few crows.

"I say, Edenhaven," the man bellowed. "Surprised to see you in this back of beyond burg. We're only here because my wife's cousin is celebrating her seventieth birthday, and the old bird refuses to travel. Hasn't spread her wings in fifty years. My wife's her heir, so we do what must be done. Eh?"

He chortled heartily at his witticism.

Adolphus gave a barely civil nod, the contours of his face carved in granite.

"Montjoy. Miss Montjoy."

"We're staying at Trammels' Restaurant and Hotel." Miss Montjoy wrinkled her nose as if she smelled fresh horse droppings. "It's provincial and bucolic but better than Aunt's rustic house. What can one expect from a dreary little seashore town that smells of fish?"

It does not smell of fish.

Aurelie took an involuntary sniff.

Sea and salt and sand, yes.

Fish, no.

"My lands," Miss Montjoy blathered on. "I cannot conceive why anyone would wish to live here. I should die of boredom within a fortnight. Why, I didn't even see a proper milliner, perfumer, or glover when we passed through yesterday."

Aurelie's already low opinion of the twit took another dive and settled somewhere in the ocean floor's depths.

Miss Montjoy scooted to the conveyance's side and, in a brazen seductress's wiliness, pressed her chest against it, causing her breasts to thrust upward. If she sneezed or if a slight breeze happened by, her bosom would pop loose of its meager confines.

Wouldn't that give the tattlemongers something to bandy about?

To Adolphus's credit, he didn't spare her overt display of feminine flesh a single glance.

However, the tongue-wagging biddies down the lane made no attempt to hide their blatant eavesdropping.

"You simply must join us for supper, my lord," Miss Montjoy cooed, fashioning her mouth into a moue and batting her eyelashes again.

A consummate flirt.

Aurelie hovered like a shy dove, afraid to move lest she draw attention to herself and yet disinclined to stay and overhear their discussion. What she'd learned already sat like curdled milk in her belly.

"Yes, yes. A brilliant notion, Gwenda, my pet." Her father patted her shoulder. "Far too little *haut ton* refinement and company in these parts."

The man must be hard of hearing. His trumpeting entranced the gossips who'd unabashedly settled in to watch the exchange—probably the most entertainment they'd had in ages.

"Could do with a bit of blue-blooded conversation," Montjoy boomed. "Seems the locals only want to chat about smuggling, fish, and ships."

Did the Montjoys have any notion how pompous and disparaging they sounded?

Likely, neither cared a whit.

"I'm in town for business." Adolphus slid Aurelie, still rooted to the stoop, an undiscernible glance. Was that remorse in his brown eyes? An apology too? "I regret I'm not accepting invitations at present."

He didn't sound the least regretful but rather taciturn.

Eyes narrowed, Miss Montjoy directed an antagonistic glance toward Aurelie. If her eyes had been daggers, they would've pinned Aurelie to the door.

Adolphus touched his hat. "If you'll excuse me, I have an appointment. I'm already late."

Because he'd taken the time to chat with Aurelie.

Despite the uncomfortable circumstances, her heart swelled with pleasure.

He strode down the street without a backward glance, and Aurelie took the opportunity to slip inside the cottage. She leaned against the closed door, her heart beating a frantic staccato and the blood whooshing in her ears.

A moment later, the clacking of the carriage's fancy painted wheels proclaimed the Montjoys had also departed.

Adolphus *was* a lord.

A marquess, to be precise.

Aurelie's stomach toppled over itself, and she pressed a shaking hand to her middle.

Did that mean he was also heir to the Latham dukedom?

THIRTEEN

SEVERAL HOURS LATER ~ A FEW MINUTES PAST ONE IN THE MORNING

Head throbbing like mules kicking the inside of his skull from too much inferior ale, too much cheap cigar smoke, and the incessant din at the Puddle Duck Tavern, Adolphus slipped inside the blessedly quiet cottage. A single, turned-down lamp glowed on the hall table. His meeting with the shipbuilder and carpenters had gone long, and he'd ended up dining on greasy stew, stale bread, and questionable cheese at the pub.

Dressed finer than most other patrons, Adolphus had become the object of attention for several of the tavern's tarts. He'd turned down no fewer than four ladybirds' invitations to go upstairs and "have a spot o' fun."

For certain, the dockside tavern was not for the faint of heart.

His stomach mightn't ever be the same.

As his rotten luck would have it, Roland Trammel swaggered in just as one aggressive and buxom strumpet had draped her fleshy arms around Adolphus's neck from behind, pushing her enormous breasts into his back. She'd reeked of sweat, cabbage, garlic, and an unwashed body.

Not an inviting combination, particularly after his unappetizing meal.

Adolphus had quickly sent *Angel*—surely not her real name—on her way, but not before Trammel invited himself to join Adolphus.

With the boss present, the ladies of the evening descended on the table like flies on sweetcakes, each hoping to earn his favor for the evening. Trammel's reputation as a rake was well deserved, and the bounder wasn't particularly selective when it came to bed sport. This evening, he'd dismissed the prostitutes with a cruel coldness that had stirred pity in Adolphus.

Trammel saw the women as property, assets, good for one thing—making him money. All right, two things— satiating his physical pleasure too.

Lifting the lamp from its resting place, Adolphus headed toward his bedchamber at the cottage's rear.

Trammel, the cocksure blighter, had also had the unmitigated gall to ask all matter of prying questions about Aurelie.

As if he dared think himself worthy of her.

A monk who'd taken a vow of silence would have revealed more than Adolphus did tonight.

Every protective instinct he possessed and no small amount of jealousy kept him mute. He'd evaded Trammel's inquisition by claiming he knew nothing about his French neighbor. For certain, what little he did know, he wasn't sharing with the dissolute bounder.

Trammel, either completely obtuse or simply an arrogant ponce, had declared he intended to call upon Aurelie. Which meant—blast Adolphus's confounded luck to the lowest level of hell—he was obliged to warn her.

And that, though well-intentioned, he was positive she would not appreciate.

Nevertheless, he would speak with her as he did not doubt that the rotter's intentions weren't honorable.

"He'll have to get past me first," Adolphus snarled to the quivering shadows on the walls.

If Trammel insisted on pursuing Aurelie, he might find himself staring down the end of a pistol or the tip of a sword on a field of honor.

Adolphus released a snort worthy of a stallion as he opened his bedchamber door.

Now he had assigned himself as Aurelie's protector?

After setting the lamp down, he disrobed, leaving only his unfastened trousers sagging at his waist as he padded to the porcelain washstand painted with a seashore landscape. Once he'd cleansed his teeth and washed his face, he blew the lamp out, kicked off his trousers, and lay atop his counterpane in his small clothes.

It was too warm to slip beneath the sheets.

An odd popping noise drew his attention to the open window.

It echoed again, and all at once, Adolphus realized what he heard. Heart lodged in his throat and icy sweat springing out on his body, he leaped from his bed. Dreading what he would see, he stuck his head out the window.

Mother of God.

"Fire!" he roared, springing from his bed.

"Fire," he shouted again, stuffing his legs into his discarded trousers. "Mason. Tilly. Mrs. Fieldstone. Sound the alarm. The roof is burning on the cottage next to Candle Glow Cottage."

He crammed his bare feet into his boots.

Aurelie!

He must warn Aurelie and her family.

Not sparing the time to don a shirt, he sprinted down the corridor, his boots thudding a hollow warning on the wood.

Hurry. Hurry. Hurry.

His house servants stood at the entrance, fear and uncertainty stamped upon their faces.

"Pound on doors," he ordered. "Wake the residents up. Notify the volunteer firefighters."

A fire could decimate an entire neighborhood in mere minutes. Adolphus shuddered, recalling the stories about the Great Fire of London in 1666, which had destroyed four-fifths of the city.

It seemed as if time stood still as he charged to the cottage next door and banged on the door.

"Fire, Aurelie. Wake up."

Please wake up. Please.

I cannot lose you.

There wasn't time to examine that epiphany now, but when this crisis was over, Adolphus intended to scrutinize the revelation.

"Aurelie." He repeatedly slammed his fists against the wood, breaking the skin on his knuckles.

When there wasn't a response, he put his shoulder to the door and tried to break it down.

Panicked cries carried to him from within the cottage.

Other terrified residents streamed into the street, and shrieks of "Fire" echoed up and down the lane. The tinny bell of the volunteer fire brigade sounded in the distance.

Thank God, but would the firefighters arrive in time to contain the inferno?

"We have a well," one man called across the street. "Bring your buckets. Hurry."

Every second counted, and these townspeople knew how quickly this blaze could consume all their homes.

Frantic with fear, Adolphus glanced around for something—*anything, Lord, there must be something*—to break a window.

He spied a metal watering can and didn't hesitate to seize the heavy container and smash the nearest window. Just as he was about to climb through the glass, the front door burst open with such force that it banged against the house.

Hair hanging around her shoulders and wearing only her thin night shift, Aurelie dragged Nathalie and a limping Rémi by the hands. Tabitha plowed through the doorway, continuing until she hung over the stone fence, gulping air.

"Take them," Aurelie gasped, shoving the sobbing, distraught children out the door toward him. "I must save Aunt Marie."

Impossible.

He would not allow it.

Permitting Aurelie to maneuver the feeble woman into her invalid chair and steer the clumsy apparatus down the corridor with the house on the verge of igniting any moment was unthinkable.

Aurelie spun around, but Adolphus grabbed her arm before she could take a step.

"I'll get your aunt, Aurelie. Stay out here. The children need you. Where is her bedroom?"

The stubborn tilt of her chin suggested she was about to argue.

There wasn't time to bicker.

"I can carry her, Aurelie. You cannot."

Indecision swept her face before she gave a grudging nod. "The back of the house, on the right side."

Most of these cottages had similar floor plans.

Adolphus should have no problem finding her.

Getting the invalid out, however?

That would prove a challenge.

He spared the cottage next door the briefest glance. Flames engulfed the entire roof, and flying sparks had ignited not only Aurelie's roof, but two other cottages, including his.

No time to worry about that now.

What mattered was saving lives.

Their faces grim but determined, townspeople carrying buckets streamed toward the conflagration.

"Do not go inside *any* building until the fire is out." He grasped Aurelie's bare shoulders and stared hard into her eyes. "Do you understand? It's not safe."

"*Oui.*" Aurelie gulped, then nodded, her golden hair swirling around her shoulders.

Then to his utter surprise, she put her palm to his cheek and whispered brokenly, "Be careful, Adolphus. *Please,* be careful."

She sounded...

He forgot to breathe.

She sounded like a woman afraid for the man she loved.

Could she hold him in a degree of affection? They'd only met a handful of times.

Was it possible?

Yes, because something foreign had awakened in him as well. Something potent and undefinable but which kept Aurelie in his thoughts even when he ought to be concentrating on other things.

The chaos around them faded: the horrified screams and cries, the clanging brigade bell, the firefighters' hoarse shouts...

Such potent emotion welled in his throat that Adolphus didn't trust himself to speak. Now wasn't the time, in any event. Instead, he gave a terse dip of his chin before diving into the cottage's gloomy interior.

He'd examine Aurelie's declaration as intently as his revelation when the time came.

Cloying smoke from the fire next door already filtered inside Candle Glow Cottage.

"Mrs. Millard? Where are you?"

"I'm here," came a feeble cry. "I cannot find Antoinette."

Adolphus shoved the door open, and the miserable cat bolted past his legs.

So much for loyalty. Unlike dogs, cats weren't known for their devotion.

"She's escaped, Mrs. Millard. She'll likely hide until the bedlam subsides. I shall have to carry you outside. We must hurry."

Without waiting for permission, he scooped the elderly woman into his arms, grunting at her unexpected weight.

She threw her arms around his neck and buried her face in his shoulder. "I thought I was going to die."

"No such thing," he assured her.

They might both perish if he didn't hurry.

Gritting his teeth against the scorching cinders dropping onto his head and bare shoulders, Adolphus moved as swiftly as he could toward the entrance while keeping an eye on the shattered windows facing the burning building next door. Timbers creaked and groaned, and a loud, distraught chorus rang outside as the cottage roof collapsed, sending flaming boards like exploding missiles into Candle Glow Cottage.

He ducked and stumbled, nearly losing his footing and dumping his burden on the floor.

Mrs. Millard squealed in terror.

"Almost there," he soothed.

At last, he burst through the doorway, his heavy burden straining his arms and his lungs burning from inhaling smoke. Coughing, he blinked stinging, watery eyes as he searched for Aurelie and the children.

A pair of weeping older women—the Branderson sisters—clung to one another. A few feet farther along the lane stood the Heddacocks, despair etched on their thin features, their four small children huddled beside them. The fire had begun in their cottage.

At least everyone had managed to make it outside to safety.

"Over here, Adolphus."

He pivoted toward Aurelie's voice.

Nathalie and Rémi clung to her. She'd procured a stool and indicated he should place her aunt on the humble piece. His arms screeching from the strain of carrying the woman, he did so and then planted his hands on his hips. Mouth taut, he surveyed the turbulent scene.

The townsfolk had split into two groups, concentrating on saving the cottages not on fire and leaving the other four to burn themselves out, including Adolphus's, Aurelie's, the Brandersons', and the Heddacocks'.

His sanctuary would likely be nothing but a pile of charred timbers come morning, as would Candle Glow Cottage.

Though it dismayed him, he wasn't overwrought. He

had other houses, clothing, and an abundance of resources.

The same wasn't true of the others who'd lost their homes tonight. Adolphus strongly suspected everything Aurelie and the children owned was in the cottage, save the bed clothing they wore.

"What is to become of us, Aunt Aurelie?" Nathalie turned huge, fear-filled eyes to her aunt. "We have nothing and nowhere to live again."

Again?

"I don't know, chérie." Aurelie bit her trembling lower lip as she hugged the shaking children to her sides. "I'll think of something. We'll get through this."

She didn't sound the least convincing, and her waxen face and enormous, worried gray eyes revealed she hadn't any idea what she would do.

He wanted to scoop her into his arms and promise her everything would be all right. To kiss the little worry lines at the corners of her eyes and mouth away. Promise that she needn't fear about her future or the children's any longer. That he would care for them from now on.

But now was not the time.

Adolphus squatted and took Nathalie's hand, then clasped Rémi's too. "I don't want you to fret about that right now. I promise, I shall take care of you."

And the others now homeless.

Although the altruistic gesture would expose his true

identity, it was the right thing to do for this little town that had brought him so much peace and joy.

"How?" Nathalie scrunched her tear-stained face. She pointed to his cottage and, voice wavering, said, "Your cottage is on fire too."

Adolphus glanced upward to find Aurelie regarding him, her expression a mixture of appreciation and consternation.

He might as well tell them.

The truth would out soon enough now.

His smile was as much self-deprecating and wistful as comforting.

"Because, sweetheart," he captured Aurelie's gaze with his. "I'm the Marquess of Edenhaven, heir to the Latham dukedom."

"I knew it," she whispered, stricken. "I knew it."

He'd expected surprise and perhaps even joy and excitement. Not devastation. "It's only a title."

"No." She shook her head, and that beautiful golden hair swished over her ivory shoulders. "It changes everything."

FOURTEEN

Trammels' Restaurant and Hotel

HOURS LATER—JUST PAST DAWN

Aurelie shoved a smoky strand of gritty hair off her face while clutching the knitted red shawl someone had draped over her shoulders in the past few hours. Barefoot and too worried to feel embarrassed as the disapproving clerk took in her shoddy appearance before procuring a key to a chamber, she kept her gaze pointed straight ahead.

Keeping her attention fixated on the ocean landscape painting served another purpose too.

It prevented her from peeking at the intriguing dark thatch of Adolphus's hair visible through his partially buttoned shirt collar. Last night, she'd seen the fascinating mat covering his chest and abdomen before narrowing and disappearing into his trousers' waistband. It caused her to curl her hands against the illogical urge to run her fingertips through the crisp, curly hair.

The clerk shot a less than accommodating glance toward the bedraggled Branderson sisters before his focus alighted on the harrowed Heddacocks, and although his mouth tightened minutely, he nodded.

Adolphus had not only arranged a suite for her family and Tabitha but rooms for his servants and the other families whose homes had succumbed to the inferno. Although a few other cottages sustained minor damage, the firefighters and the townsfolk hailed the heroic efforts as a success.

No one denied the loss of four cottages was tragic, but everyone understood the outcome could've been far worse. At least no one had died.

Her head ached—the temples pounding mercilessly—from apprehension, smoke, and the tumult of the past few hours. She glanced downward, her filthy toes peeking from beneath her night rail's dirty and frayed hem.

Beneath the cover of the shawl, she fingered the slight bump near her hip beneath her nightgown. She'd managed to pin her sapphire brooch to the underside before racing to the children's room. That single piece of jewelry was all that stood between them and the poor house. The thought of pawning the memento caused hot tears to sting her eyes, but she had no choice now.

"Baths for everyone. Food too." Adolphus gave the orders with the ease of someone accustomed to having his demands met. He glanced downward and gave her a reassuring smile. "Clothing, shoes, hair brushes... all the essentials. Put everything on my bill."

"Yes, your lordship." The clerk scribbled away, nodding in deference.

A future duke had never graced the hotel with his imperious presence before. While the staff couldn't quite conceal their disdain for the exhausted, grimy patrons awaiting rooms, they didn't dare offend someone of Adolphus's station.

Aurelie hadn't even had the time to process that he was a lord—a future duke.

He'd risked his life to save Aunt Marie, who now sat on a luxurious plum-colored chair, clutching Antoinette in her arms.

When the clerk had insisted no animals were permitted in the guest rooms, Adolphus had merely raised a superior eyebrow, and the spineless fellow had conceded as readily as a candle melting on a blazing hearth.

She couldn't imagine having that much power and influence. How easily one might abuse both if one were a blackguard.

Adolphus touched her arm, dragging her back to the

present. "Bathe, eat, and sleep. I've arranged to have clothing and toiletries delivered to your suite. We'll talk this afternoon. I have several things I must see to."

"You need to sleep too." Dark shadows accented his brown eyes. He sported several angry crimson burn marks on his face and neck. She'd seen many more on his broad shoulders and back before a kind stranger had given him a humble shirt to don.

With sincere thanks, he'd done so without hesitation.

He'd unraveled everything she believed about the nobility, leaving her adrift. Aurelie's tightly held beliefs that all aristocrats and royalty were unconscionable, self-serving fiends dissolved in the wake of his sacrifice, decency, and honor.

She cocked her head, studying him as he spoke in low tones to the clerk.

He confused her.

Mesmerized her too.

Why had he chosen to live anonymously when most peers paraded around like proud roosters? For certain, those she'd known in France had—the pompous braggarts, full of their own self-importance.

Aurelie had no choice but to accept Adolphus's help, but this arrangement was temporary—a day or two at most.

She almost moaned aloud but wouldn't let the children see her despair.

What *was* she going to do?

Where would they live?

How could she replace their clothing and other possessions?

Her mind balked at facing those troubling questions at this moment.

It was simply too much to consider, and all Aurelie wanted to do was crawl into a clean bed and cry herself to sleep. So, though it grated on her independence and conscience, she'd let Adolphus take on the responsibility for the short term, for she hadn't the strength to do it anymore.

Oh, she'd recover. Aurelie was resilient after all, but losing everything one possessed did rather take the wind out of one's sails. And when one was responsible for three other people...?

She sighed, feeling more forlorn and hopeless than when Gaston died. Then, there'd been the hope of a new life in England. Now...?

She couldn't imagine a future.

Couldn't envision a future where her nearest neighbor wasn't a frustratingly enigmatic, tantalizingly handsome, and wholly tempting man. Not a peer or aristocrat, nor a lord or duke. Just a man with a seductive and melodic baritone on the other side of a brick wall which—for a short time—made her hope for things she'd stopped yearning for.

Half-turning, she met Aunt Marie's fretful gaze.

Someone had acquired an invalid chair for her.

Uncertainty glinted in the depths of her eyes as she no doubt understood their situation's graveness. Her meager widow's annual allowance couldn't begin to cover housing, clothing, and everything required to establish a household. Returning to Stratham-Whiteley wasn't a better option since the house was far too costly to maintain.

Aurelie shifted her focus to Nathalie and Rémi, sagging against each other on another armchair. The precious darlings struggled to keep their eyes open between wide yawns.

Tabitha dozed on a nearby sofa, her mouth hanging open. She'd already tearfully informed Aurelie and Aunt Marie that she planned to return to her village on the first mail coach headed in that direction. Hopefully, on the morrow.

"You there." Adolphus caught the eye of a bellboy. "Please push Mrs. Millard's chair."

No point in waking Tabitha as her duties had ended.

The spry fellow trotted over to grasp the handles as Adolphus lifted Rémi in one arm and took Nathalie's hand. "Let's see your rooms, shall we?"

Giving him weary nods, they produced tremulous smiles.

Once inside their elegant suite—Aurelie didn't want to imagine the cost—they revived a bit, charging to the table to gobble the breakfast laid out for them with grimy hands. Even Aunt Marie dove into the food like she hadn't eaten in a week.

Aurelie didn't have the strength to admonish the children to wash their hands before eating or chastise them for stuffing food in their mouths. Neither issue seemed all that important after the night's tragedy.

Antoinette lifted her tail and inspected every piece of furniture with her typical disdain before selecting an armchair and jumping onto the cushion. She kneaded the tuft with her needle-like claws for a few seconds before curling into a ball to sleep—her nose beneath her tail.

As Aurelie made to slip inside, eager for a bath and a bite to eat herself, Adolphus caught her hand.

She gave him a questioning glance before gently withdrawing her hand. She knew her place, and allowing a future duke to hold her hand suggested a relationship she wasn't willing to enter into.

You may have no choice.

Could she do it?

Become his mistress to put food on the table and ensure her family had somewhere to live?

For how long, though?

Was the current crisis worth surrendering her virtue over?

Putting the pony before the cart, aren't you, Aurelie Dominique Eugenie Lemieux? Adolphus hasn't so much as hinted that he desires a clandestine arrangement. You do him an injustice.

"I'm sorry I didn't tell you who I was." A wry grin tipped his sculpted lips upward, an attractive contrast to his chiseled, soot-smudged jaw. A small, angry blister had formed on his upper lip where a spark must've landed. "Though I suspect you discerned the truth yourself."

Clasping her hands before her, she shrugged.

"It is your business, my lord. I'm sure you had your reasons."

His secrecy shouldn't hurt.

It made no sense that it did.

But nothing had made much sense since Adolphus Westbrook, Marquess of Edenhaven, had burst into her life.

"Tut. None of that." He shook a finger before Aurelie's face, though his boyish smile belied any true rebuke. "It's Adolphus. I've only ever been Adolphus to you and only ever shall be."

His voice had grown husky and deep, and she found his declaration disturbingly touching. More of that tenderness, and she'd be clay in his hands.

She summoned a kernel of common sense.

"It's not proper. People will talk." They already were. "I'd spare the children further gossip."

He drew his brows together. "Yes. I hadn't considered that."

That was all she considered these days.

"Come, Auntie. There are fresh blueberries." Nathalie held up a navy-blue berry before popping it into her mouth and chewing happily.

"I'll be there in a minute." Aurelie was so hungry, her belly button gnawed at her spine. It seemed a calamity stirred everyone's appetites.

"I must run a few errands including making living arrangements for the other families who lost their homes until the cottages can be rebuilt, but I insist we speak when I return, Aurelie."

Even in the ill-fitting shirt, with soot smudged on his chin and left cheek, Adolphus was the most handsome man she'd ever seen. He bore his nobility with a mystifying nonchalance.

Weary as she was, she couldn't prevent the droll smile that tipped her lips upward.

"Already insisting, your lordship? My, you've fallen into your old habits quite easily now that you've revealed your true identity."

Disquiet flickered across his face.

"Please, Aurelie, will you agree to meet with me?"

That this proud, powerful man deigned to ask her with what appeared to be genuine earnestness did something dangerous to her heart.

Be careful, Aurelie.

He's not for you.

No, he was not.

If Adolphus had been a commoner, she might've held a tinge of hope. But there was no room in her life for Adolphus, the lord and future duke, or more on point, in his life for her.

"Of course." She managed a passably pleasant smile. "Shall we say three in the restaurant?"

Though what she'd wear, she could not imagine.

"Perfect." He grinned, that flash of white teeth that hitched the air in her lungs and made her knees weak. Then he brought her hand to his mouth and kissed her knuckles, and after budding like a rose in the summer sun, another piece of her traitorous heart plopped to his feet.

Mon Dieu.

She stood in the doorway, gazing down the empty corridor long after he'd disappeared.

That man could break her heart—*would* break her heart—if she didn't protect it well.

FIFTEEN

Trammels' Restaurant

QUARTER TO FOUR THAT AFTERNOON

Aurelie was late.

Adolphus glanced toward the restaurant's opulent entrance for the umpteenth time. Decorated in the same garish gold, crimson, and black as the hotel, he supposed the overdone décor might appeal to some. The potted Ficus and ferns were tolerable, but the interior resembled a gaming hell house of ill-repute he'd visited several years ago.

He'd arrived fifteen minutes early this afternoon and spent the last hour rehearsing what he wanted to say to Aurelie. A pessimistic grin tried to wrest his mouth upward, but he forced the intractable smirk into submission. More than one curious diner cast furtive glances in his direction. He didn't need them speculating why he grinned to himself like a lunatic.

Besides, despite his outer composure, rare uncertainty riddled him.

He, the future Duke of Latham, fretted he couldn't convince Aurelie to accept the offer he intended to make. She'd refuse at first, of course. After all, she was proud and self-reliant—traits he admired about her. But those qualities wouldn't put food on the table or keep a roof over her family's heads.

He was confident that she would see things his way in the end.

Adolphus was no fool, nor was he ignorant of the ways of the world and how particularly harsh and cruel life was to a woman without means or station.

He fingered the handle of the knife.

Yes, Aurelie would eventually accept, though likely grudgingly at first. Until then, he must convince her to permit him to pay for her and her family's hotel room. He hoped that because he also provided for the others, it would bolster his argument that she should accept.

"*My lord*," trilled a familiar sing-song voice. *Bollocks.* "What an unexpected surprise."

Hardly unexpected as everyone in the township knew those whose cottages were destroyed currently stayed at the hotel. And since Adolphus had requested the most discreet table in the farthest corner, Gwenda Montjoy had to wend her way through the other occupied tables like a hound on the scent to reach him.

Glancing upward, he stiffened as she bore down upon him like a runaway coach and four. He searched behind her in vain for her father. No reprieve there. *Blast and damn.* If the impudent chit thought to join him, he'd soon disavow her of that rattlepated notion.

As was her wont, she wore a lavender gown, this one trimmed in violet and jade green. A jaunty purple feather accented her perfectly coiffed dark hair, and amethysts glittered at her ears.

"Miss Montjoy." He motioned the approaching waiter, intent on seating her away, earning Adolphus a pout from the spoiled beauty and a confused frown from the eager fellow.

Her brown eyes flashed with annoyance before she fashioned a coquette's smile.

"Might I join you?" She placed her lavender-gloved hands on the back of the chair beside Adolphus's. "Papa's gout acted up, and he's resting."

Drumming his fingertips on the table, Adolphus leaned back.

"Alas, I have no one to take tea with." Her artificial smile narrowed her cat-like eyes.

One. Two. Three.

As if on cue, she batted her eyelashes and struck a coy poise.

And there it was.

Was there anything authentic or spontaneous about Gwenda Montjoy?

"I am sorry to hear Montjoy isn't feeling well. However, I am expecting a guest. I am sure you understand."

He'd rather gargle hot coals and ride bare-arsed naked on a thistle blanket than have to endure the simpering, pampered twit's company. Brushing his fingertips along the table's edge, Adolphus gave her a bland stare, enjoying the play of emotions across her face as she digested his not-entirely-polite refusal.

Disbelief. Annoyance. Offense. Shrewdness. And then, dawning comprehension.

An unbecoming sneer curled her rouged lips as she jerked her chin upward in haughty offense.

How different she was from Aurelie in looks and temperament, which was no doubt why he couldn't abide Gwenda Montjoy's company but relished time spent with Aurelie.

"It's that common, lowborn chit from the cottage next to yours, isn't it? I saw the way she ogled you the other day. Couldn't tear her gaze from you, the brazen slattern."

Is that a fact?

Most interesting.

Adolphus very nearly permitted himself a smug smile.

Miss Montjoy gave an artificial laugh, the sound rather like cats mating or crystal breaking. She glanced around and smirked all the more when she observed others keenly watching the tense exchange.

Likely, she'd been snooping around and asking questions about Aurelie.

"I never believed I'd see the day when you entertained someone so far beneath your touch, Edenhaven. I'm sure it's not a coincidence that you have the cottage next to hers. A most *convenient* arrangement, to be sure."

The jealous shrew showed her true colors for everyone to see. It painted Miss Montjoy in a very unflattering light.

Adolphus merely raised an eyebrow.

There was no way in all of Christendom he would address her crude and repulsive accusations.

What was it Shakespeare had said?

Methinks ye doth protest too much?

Yes, and denial inevitably made things worse.

Across the restaurant, Trammel observed the exchange with bored indifference.

When Adolphus remained impassive to her spiteful tirade, Miss Montjoy sidled nearer and leaned down, giving him a harlot's view of her unimpressive bosom.

"You've truly lowered your standards, my lord."

With deliberate slowness, he curled his fingers around

his wineglass and lifted it. Before taking a sip, he murmured, low but perfectly enunciated so that everyone within ten feet could hear his every word.

"Not so low that I would ever invite *you* to dine at my table."

A collective gasp rent the air as his target hit home.

Miss Montjoy's jaw sagged open wide enough for an albatross to nest in before she snapped her mouth shut with an audible click. Piercing him with a murderous glare, she turned on her expensive heels and stormed across the restaurant, muttering obscenities beneath her breath.

Only the lush carpet kept her heels from impaling the innocent floor with each livid step.

Every patron in the restaurant watched her progress with macabre fascination. It wasn't often a member of the *haut ton* behaved so poorly in public. In private, however, it was an entirely different matter.

Aurelie entered the restaurant, coming to an uncertain stop as she discerned something was afoot.

He stood so she could see him.

Her hesitant gaze sought his across the spans, and he sent her a brilliant, welcoming smile.

Every time Adolphus saw her, his heart took flight, his blood humming in his veins. She was balm to his soul, light to his spirit, and he craved her presence as a sailor craved his rum.

Accustomed to rigid self-control, this newfound liberation took a bit of getting used to. But Adolphus liked it—liked it a great deal, in truth. He wasn't going to affect indifference when it came to Aurelie.

Let tongues wag from now until next Season.

He didn't give a beggar's curse.

Back inflexible with suppressed rage, Miss Montjoy charged forth like a demented rhinoceros straight toward Aurelie.

Surely, she wouldn't cause further public embarrassment.

On second thought, that was exactly the sort of thing a spoiled, cossetted chit like Gwenda Montjoy would do.

Adolphus stepped forward, prepared to protect Aurelie from the seething shrew, but Trammel arrived at her side first. Acting as a physical barrier, he stepped between the women and placed Aurelie's hand on his arm.

It should be Adolphus acting the chivalrous hero. Jealousy twisted her jagged blade deep in his gut. A novel sensation and one he wasn't certain how to dispel.

"*You. You.*" Miss Montjoy sputtered, so overwrought she couldn't cobble a coherent sentence together. "You upstart—"

"Enough, Miss Montjoy. You are disturbing my guests."

Trammel's stern visage and flint-like eyes gave the seething woman pause.

A vision in light pink, her hair artfully arranged atop her head, Aurelie retreated a step and regarded Miss Montjoy with the wariness one did a provoked cobra about to strike.

Wise on her part.

It had taken no small amount of cajoling and a hefty bribe to have the gown that had been commissioned for another delivered to her. Nevertheless, it had been the only finished pink gown Adolphus could find in Lymington. That he wanted to please her by providing a gown in her favorite color said much about how far she'd wiggled her way past his reinforced barricades.

With only two local seamstresses available, the frock was not patterned after a Paris fashion plate. No doubt *le beau monde* would consider the garment plain and unimpressive. Though loose in the waist and a trifle short for Aurelie's five-foot-seven frame, the pilfered gown fit relatively well.

However, what the flattering shade did to Aurelie's creamy skin and gray eyes should've been illegal. It made him consider what the rest of her ivory skin might look like, and those musings did unmentionable things to his libido.

Several men eyed her with something more than casual interest, and a couple of sots assessed her feminine attributes with such boldness that he balled his fists at his sides.

Future dukes did not plant gentleman facers, even if the lecherous fiends deserved to be knocked into next December.

At Trammel's discreet nod, the concierge and a waiter flanked Miss Montjoy on either side, forcing her, still complaining shrilly, from the restaurant.

Aurelie visibly relaxed, though she watched until the other woman disappeared.

She met Adolphus's eyes across the distance, a question in hers.

What was Miss Montjoy to him?

SIXTEEN

Still in Trammel's Restaurant

TWO HEARTBEATS LATER

God pity the poor chap who married that harpy —heiress or not.

At once, excited tittering and whispers buzzed around the establishment.

"Miss Lemieux, please permit me to escort you to your table." A grin bordering on gloating framing his mouth, Trammel extended his elbow as he looked his fill of her bosom.

Taken aback, Aurelie reluctantly placed her fingertips on his forearm, and he sent Adolphus a superior smirk.

Adolphus would bet his title the rotter had never

personally offered a guest so much as a glass of water before today. No, this was all an act, as much to thwart Miss Montjoy as to further his suit. The bounder had seen an opportunity and seized it with the finesse of a practiced pickpocket.

Regardless, if Trammel didn't keep his focus above Aurelie's neck and wipe the satisfied smile off his face, Adolphus would plant his fist in Trammel's too-straight nose—honor and decorum be hanged.

Aurelie cast an unnerved glance toward Adolphus.

He strode forward to answer her silent request.

"There you are, my dear." He made certain the gawkers heard the endearment and took great satisfaction in Trammel's scowl.

Pink tinged Aurelie's cheeks, but her eyes softened at the corners, and she fashioned a sweet smile. "I fear I over-slept. Please excuse my tardiness."

"It is of no consequence." He stepped forward, forcing Trammel to halt. "I'll escort Miss Lemieux from here, Trammel."

"I think not, Edenhaven." Trammel's voice and face took on a flint-like edge. "I've wanted the opportunity to become better acquainted with Miss Lemieux, and as she is a guest in my hotel, I shall see to her needs henceforth."

The implication was as clear as the spotless windows lining the front of the restaurant.

God help me not to lay him out like a rug.

Trammel's declaration caused a buzz of excitement amongst the diners.

Ashen, Aurelie jerked her hand away. "*Non*, I don't think—"

Adolphus stepped near and in a fury-laced voice murmured quietly, "Stay away from Miss Lemieux or I swear, I'll ruin you." He impaled the other man with a glare meant to incinerate him. "Do you take my meaning?"

Trammel better think long and hard about crossing him because he possessed the power to destroy the man.

Expression pinched, but unwilling to cause a scene in front of his already titillated patrons or risk Adolphus carrying out his very real threat, Trammel relinquished Aurelie to Adolphus.

She visibly relaxed when she took his arm.

Trammel made her nervous, as he ought to.

The cur would've ruined her and tossed her to the curb afterward. He'd fathered three bastards on local girls and those were only the ones Adolphus knew about. There were likely more.

"You failed to mention the wind blew in *that* direction, Edenhaven." Smirking, Trammel brushed a licentious glance over Aurelie's golden curls. "Not that I'll usually let another *ship* deter me."

Adolphus gave the other man his wintriest smile. The one that sent shivers up grown men's spines and had them hightailing to the nearest exit if they possessed an ounce of good sense.

Trammel merely raised a scoffing eyebrow in silent challenge.

He would not acquiesce without a fight. Either he was a lackwit—which Adolphus very much doubted—or he was so full of himself he wouldn't retreat.

That did not bode well for Aurelie or Trammel, for Adolphus would not be thwarted either.

"Well, the wind does blow in *that* direction." Adolphus stared the man down. Never mind that until this precise moment, he'd not admitted that very interesting fact to himself or considered what it meant for his future. "And you would be wise to sail your vessel to another port. A harbor with an open pier that would welcome you dropping anchor."

It didn't escape Adolphus how the ludicrous innuendos had steered the conversation into absurdity.

Curving his lips into a rogue's smile, Trammel gave Aurelie a short bow.

"Until later, Miss Lemieux."

The gimlet eye he turned upon Adolphus promised repercussions.

All the more reason that he must persuade Aurelie to accept his offer and remove himself and her family from Lymington for a time.

She glanced at Adolphus from the corner of her eye as he directed her to their table.

"Please tell me *that* peculiar exchange wasn't what I think it was."

After seating her next to him and pushing her chair in, Adolphus resumed his seat and flicked open his napkin. He must choose his next words with extreme care.

"Don't trouble yourself over it."

"Adolphus." Censure in her eyes, she leaned forward, the lush swells of her pert breasts rising tantalizingly high. "Did you just warn Mr. Trammel away from me?"

He should've known they hadn't fooled her a jot. "I did."

With a displeased huff, she sat back, glaring at him. "You overstepped."

"He's a rake, Aurelie. A libertine. A bounder."

With a slight lift of his chin, he indicated tea should be served.

"Trust me." He pursed his mouth. "His intentions are not honorable."

"That still does not give you the right. I am four and twenty and quite capable of defending myself." A chill had entered her tone. Her pretty gray eyes narrowed in suspicion. "*Zut.* Did you also pay for Rémi's ankle because I have not received a bill from Doctor Bresingham?"

No sense denying it.

Besides, Adolphus wanted to earn her trust.

He touched the back of her hand with two fingertips. He wished he dared cover it with his palm. "I swear, I meant to tell you, but I had to leave, and there wasn't an opportunity when I returned. I only intended to help."

A waiter approached with their tea tray. Strained and poignant silence descended as the servant expertly arranged the tea service.

Once finished, he asked, "Will there be anything else, my lord?"

Adolphus perused the trays of dainties and sweet-meats. He hadn't eaten today and was ravenous. "Sandwiches, if they are available."

"Of course, my lord." The waiter hurried away to do as bid.

When he was out of earshot, Aurelie whispered, "You are very presumptuous and audacious, my lord."

"I've been told so before." It rather came with the territory—peer and all that rot. Except Adolphus believed his stuffiness had ebbed a trifle these past weeks. Mayhap not as much as he'd have liked.

She jutted her stubborn chin out a fraction.

"I repeat, you had no right, Adolphus. Not to protect me or pay my bills. It gives people the wrong impression. What must Doctor Bresingham think?"

Did she realize she'd addressed him by his given name?

Voice lowered, Adolphus murmured, "I would make

it my right to protect and care for you and your family."
He might as well play his hand. "I have a suggestion…"

Every bit of color drained from Aurelie's face. Deathly
pale, she gripped the table's edge with white-knuckled
fingers.

She looked as if she was about to swoon.

"Aurelie?"

Whatever had made her so distraught?

"Do not, I pray, say anything further." Though each
word was a mere whisp of sound as it escaped her tight
mouth, they lashed him with the force of a two-sided
blade.

She licked her lower lip and sent a nervous glance
around the restaurant before resting those tragedy-filled
eyes on him. Despair leeched into her voice, and dismay
darkened her eyes to navy blue.

"I cannot give you the answer you seek, Adolphus."

"But you don't know exactly what I am proposing."
Regarding her, Adolphus rubbed his jaw. He'd expected
her to be upset, but this overwrought reaction didn't
make sense.

Aurelie busied herself preparing the tea with practiced
efficiency, then handed him his cup. He had no doubt she
did so to keep tongues from wagging as they continued to
be the center of attention. She stirred her tea laced with
milk before laying the spoon aside. Roving her guarded
gaze to the tables closest to them, she took a sip.

A silent reminder that anyone could overhear them.

He'd honestly believed she'd be happy about the arrangement once she knew what he had in mind. Well, perhaps not at first, but she'd come to understand it was the most practical and wisest choice in time. It would also protect her and her family from blighters like Trammel.

"It's a position of..." Her face flamed scarlet, but she forged on. *Brave little soldier.* "...employment, is it not?"

"How the blazes...?"

She was correct, but he hadn't decided for certain himself until this afternoon, so how could she possibly ascertain his intent?

He took a bite of seed cake, chewing thoughtfully.

Until he'd rebuilt his Lymington cottage—and that of the two displaced families as well— he intended to open his house in Sussex, near Hastings. He'd need a house-keeper, maids, a cook, footmen, and a butler. He'd ask his current staff if they wished to work there. If not, he'd help find them employment in the area.

With seven and thirty rooms, there was plenty of space for Nathalie, Rémi, and Mrs. Millard.

Even that obnoxious cat.

He set his fork down. "You won't consider *any* position I offer?"

He hadn't considered she'd find the notion repugnant.

Reluctance, he'd expected.

Abhorrence? No.

It did rather bruise a man's pride.

He took a sip of steaming tea, burning his tongue in the process.

Confound it.

Now he wouldn't be able to taste his sandwiches properly.

"My answer is unequivocally *non*. No," Aurelie declared with such vehemence he might've suggested she become his paramour.

Of a sudden, Adolphus understood her averseness.

Good God above.

That was exactly what Aurelie believed—that he wanted her to become his mistress.

Horror and hilarity struck him simultaneously, and he almost spewed his mouthful across the table. He swallowed the scalding brew, laughter nearly choking him.

He would've hugged her for jumping to the galling, offensive, and altogether inappropriate but hilarious conclusion if they were alone. His groin quite liked the naughtier notion and reacted with predictable virile maleness.

Did she think so little of him that she assumed his intent could only be dishonorable?

Perhaps the men in her life hadn't been honorable.

He'd never denied his attraction to Aurelie, and after

she refused to accompany him to luncheon the other day, he had reassessed his suspicions about her.

A woman bent on snaring him wouldn't have eschewed the opportunity. No, a husband-hunting, fortune-seeking opportunist would've donned her bonnet and gloves in less time than it took him to open the gate.

He credited his brother Lucius for encouraging him to give Aurelie a fair chance instead of rejecting her based on his assumptions and circumstantial evidence.

"If you are attracted to this young woman, why not let things play out instead of rejecting her outright?" When had Lucius become the wise brother? *"You might discover she is exactly what you want and need. 'Tis stupid to act upon assumptions, big brother."*

Zounds, wouldn't Lucius and their other brothers gloat over this present awkwardness? They'd howl with glee that their fussy eldest brother hadn't the finesse to hire a housekeeper without the woman involved thinking he made her an improper proposal.

He had truly lost his touch.

Perhaps because he cared so deeply for Aurelie and offering her the position was merely a means of keeping her near so that he could woo her. When the time was right, when he was confident she shared his feelings, then he'd make an entirely proper proposal.

A chuckle burbled up Adolphus's chest and escaped. Shoulders shaking, he shook his head, unable to speak.

"What, pray tell, is so amusing?" Blue fire sparked in Aurelie's eyes.

"My dear Miss Lemieux." Another chuckle interrupted him. Lord, when was the last time he'd been so amused? "I am... in need... of a..." he swiped at his eyes with the knuckles of his forefingers. "Housekeeper for my home in Hastings. That is where I intend to reside until my cottage is rebuilt."

Her eyes went wide as saucers, and her pretty mouth slackened.

"A *house...keeper...*?"

Embarrassment whisked across her face, followed by swiftly masked disappointment.

Adolphus understood the former emotion, but not the reason for the latter.

"*Your* housekeeper," she repeated. Incredulity laced the husky words as they faded away. She edged nearer and whispered for his ears alone, "Not a... Oh, good heavens. I've made an awful muddle, haven't I?"

Then, to his astonishment, her shoulders began shaking, and she giggled behind her hand. Tears of mirth welled in her eyes. "Please forgive me. I thought you..."

"I know..." He winked, thoroughly enjoying her adorable discomposure. "And I couldn't imagine what I'd done that led you to suppose such a thing."

Not that the notion of bedding the enticing Aurelie Lemieux was beyond his imagination. He just hadn't imagined the act in all of its glorious detail *yet*. And now that she'd roused the idea from dormancy, he'd probably not be able to stop thinking about it in great, creative detail. And that made him a bounder and a cad of the same ilk as Trammel.

For reasons he didn't understand, that struck Adolphus as even more hysterical.

For once in his life, Adolphus Westbrook, Marquess of Edenhaven and future Duke of Latham, cocked a snook at society and dissolved in unrestrained laughter along with Aurelie.

No doubt every patron stared in their direction, but he didn't give two groats. Or guineas or pounds.

Aurelie regained her composure first and took a demure sip of tea. Nevertheless, merriment danced in her gaze, and her lips quivered from time to time.

Later, he'd worry about how to convince her to agree. Because at this moment, he experienced more joy than he could recall, and the vivacious woman beside him was the reason. And that caused him to consider all sorts of impractical, improbable, implausible, fascinating things no future duke should ever contemplate.

"You'll give me an answer tomorrow?" he encouraged.

Aurelie gave him a long, considering look. "I shall."

Pray God it was the answer Adolphus wanted.

SEVENTEEN

Guest Suite – Trammel's Hotel

THE NEXT MORNING

Aurelie sat on the chair with her legs tucked beneath her and stared out the window. The sun had risen an hour ago, but she hadn't moved from the chair she'd occupied since the wee hours of the morning.

She'd promised Adolphus an answer by this afternoon.

Could she become his housekeeper?

The position was the solution to so many problems. In truth, Adolphus's offer was a God send.

But that meant seeing him every day. Consulting with him over household issues. Sleeping beneath the same roof.

Could she perform her duties and keep her love hidden?

She'd tried to deny her feelings—attributed them to other things. It hadn't been hard to convince herself what she felt wasn't love—until he'd risked his life to save Aunt Marie and then not only provided for Aurelie's family but for the other misplaced families too.

His intrinsic goodness, kindness, and generosity crumbled the last vestiges of her resistance.

Aurelie loved him—loved the Marquess of Edenhaven.

How could she not?

Outside, the sound of a wagon trundling over the cobblestones carried to her third-story chamber. A cirl bunting warbled a sleepy good morning.

Biting the edge of her thumbnail, she asked herself the question she'd asked dozens of times during the long night.

Could she keep her affections hidden from Adolphus?

Sighing, she uncurled her stiff legs, wincing as the blood began to circulate again and pins and needles tingled the flesh.

"I must. I have no choice."

"You must what, my dear? What haven't you any choice about?" Wearing her nightgown and robe, Aunt Marie shuffled into the sitting room, leaning heavily on her cane.

"Aunt." Aurelie leaped to her still partially numb feet. "Why didn't you call me? I could've assisted you into your chair."

Aunt Marie waved her cane back and forth. "Pish posh. I can still walk, though I'm not as spry as I once was."

She plopped onto the nearest chair, and Antoinette wasted no time leaping onto her lap.

"Now tell me, my dear. What has you talking to yourself?" Kindness brimmed in her eyes as she stroked the cat, whose loud purrs soon filled the room.

"Lord Edenhaven has offered me a housekeeping position at his home near Hastings in Sussex." She shoved her unbound hair off her shoulder. "The wages are very generous, and the house is large, so there is plenty of room for all of us."

She crossed to take her aunt's frail hand, then bent and kissed her papery cheek. "His lordship said you, the children, and Antoinette are welcome. It's an answer to our prayers. I know it is. We'd not have to worry about finances any longer."

"And yet you hesitate?" Aunt Marie tugged Aurelie's hand. "Sit down, child. Tell me what you are afraid of."

Aurelie lifted her gaze to meet her aunt's warm regard. "I have done something utterly stupid. Beyond the pale." Averting her gaze, she bit her lip. "I tried not to. I really did."

"You love the marquess." Compassion and empathy threaded Aunt Marie's statement.

Aurelie jerked her attention to her aunt.

"Is it that obvious?" she whispered, mortified to think she was so transparent.

"Tut. Not at all." She shook her head, still covered with her nightcap. "Only to someone who knows you well."

Relief washed over her.

Antoinette stretched and chirped, giving Aurelie a *why-are-you-talking-when-I-want-to-sleep* look.

She swept her hand over the cat, earning an approving hum.

"Adolphus mustn't know, Aunt Marie. Promise you'll keep my secret."

Aunt Marie took a deep breath and released it with a long sigh. "I shall, of course. I'm an old woman and may not have the right of it. But from the first time I met his lordship, I couldn't help but notice the way he looked at you. Are you sure you don't want him to know? He might return your regard. I would see you happy, my dear."

The smile that tipped Aurelie's mouth upward held no joy. "He's a future duke. I'm but a mere French *emigrante.* Our worlds are too far apart. I know that. *Oui,* he must marry someone of his own station. I shall have to be satisfied with tending his house."

"Noble blood runs in your veins too, Aurelie. Do not forget your mother was a distant cousin of the queen."

Aurelie adored her aunt for trying to make her feel better. Squaring her shoulders, she raised her chin. "We have no recourse. I must accept his offer. I want to. At least I can be with him."

"And when he marries, for you know he must?" Though the question was gentle, it skewered Aurelie's heart.

The pain so eviscerated her that she couldn't speak for a moment.

Of course, Adolphus must marry.

And she must provide for her family.

Fate didn't give either of them a choice in those matters.

Drawing on her resilience, she shoved her hair behind her again. "Lord Edenhaven shan't reside at Hawkshead Court full time. Once he becomes the duke, I'm sure he'll spend the majority of his time elsewhere. He's only opening the house because of his cottage burning here."

Aunt Marie gave her a look that said she wasn't as confident that was the reason as Aurelie was.

If only there were truth to her speculation.

"Then it's settled." Aurelie rose. "I shall tell his lordship this afternoon that we gladly accept his generous offer."

And somehow, she would manage to hide the secret her heart held and try not to die from a broken heart when he married another.

EIGHTEEN

Hawkshead Court, Near Hastings, Sussex

SIXTEEN DAYS LATER ~ 4 JUNE ~ LATE AFTERNOON

Humming beneath her breath, Aurelie inspected the newly opened and cleaned green garden-themed salon. Though faded from its former glory, pretty floral silk wallpaper depicting garden scenes festooned two walls. Sparkling beveled glass windows, swathed in forest green velvet draperies tied back with gold ropes, occupied a third, and an immense double door painted with *tromp-l'oeil* fountains dominated the fourth.

She rearranged a couple of the pink roses, just so, in

the cerulean blue Vulliamy vase on the center marble-topped rosewood table, then gave a satisfied nod.

The room would do.

So far, she and the other household staff had managed to put to rights almost a third of Hawkshead Court's rooms since they'd arrived nine days ago. The furnishings, though dated, were in surprisingly decent condition.

Adolphus had insisted that she assist him in hiring the butler, four maids, two footmen, a cook, two stable hands, a gardener, and a coachman. When she'd asked about a valet for him, he'd said he'd send for his in London. None of his Lymington staff had wanted to relocate, so he'd settled funds on them until they could find new positions.

Each day she fell further in love with Adolphus. She'd sometimes catch him observing her with a smoldering intensity she didn't understand. He'd smile and turn away as if he hadn't scorched her to her core, leaving her hot and confused.

No one ever told her love was a perplexing, muddled, happy torment. It was at once both the most splendid thing and the most maddening.

Rémi slipped into the room and slid his hand into hers. "Aunt Aurelie?"

"*Oui,* darling?" She needed to consider whether she would continue acting as the children's tutor or if she should hire a governess for them. The generous salary Adolphus paid her would permit the luxury.

"It's yes, not *oui*, Auntie."

Smiling, she ruffled his dark hair. "And so it is. We are all still learning, yes?"

She searched his pinched face.

"What is it, Rémi?"

He took a deep breath, then spoke rapidly, as if he'd rehearsed his little speech many times. "Do you think his lordship would permit the stable hands to give me riding lessons?"

Surprised because he'd never shown an interest in horseflesh before, she cocked her head and touched his cheek. "You want to learn to ride?"

Zut, what little boy didn't, goose?

"Very much so." He gave a solemn nod. Such a serious little fellow. Fate had stolen much from this child and his sister.

"I would too." Nathalie hurried into the room, her yellow calico gown swirling around her ankles and brushing her black shoes, eagerness stamped upon her face. "I adore horses."

Guilt speared Aurelie.

A trifle afraid of horses, she hadn't considered how much they missed their father's stables in France. Not only had finances made it impossible to keep horseflesh, it had never occurred to her to provide them with riding lessons.

Would Adolphus think it too much of an imposition?

Gazing out the window to the tops of the stables just visible beyond the knoll, she bit her lower lip.

For certain, it was outside the bounds. Children of servants weren't permitted the same privileges as their parents' employer's offspring. Having been raised in wealth and opulence the first years of their lives, Rémi and Nathalie still hadn't quite adjusted to their impoverished lives.

Neither, in truth, had Aurelie.

"Would you ask his lordship if we could ride his horses, Aunt Aurelie?" Nathalie's plea was a trifle too perfect. "He's a nice man. I think he might agree."

He was a nice man. It warmed her heart that the children thought so too. Aunt Marie gushed over Adolphus so much that Aurelie was on the verge of forbidding her aunt—currently enjoying an afternoon nap—to speak of him.

This move had been a wise choice—her only choice. Nevertheless, Adolphus had invited them into his home and treated them like guests.

Aurelie folded her arms and fixed a gimlet eye on her niece and nephew. "How long have you been plotting and practicing to ask me to impose upon his lordship?"

Aurelie disliked asking him for anything. He'd already done so much that it chafed at her independence and conscience.

The children shared a guilty look.

"Since last week when the horses arrived," Remi admitted.

Adolphus had arranged for a half dozen beautiful steppers to stable at his estate. Horses he'd boarded at the ducal country seat, but they might as well stay here now. Didn't that portend he planned on residing at Hawkshead Court for some time then?

"I shall ask his lordship if you can have lessons. I shall pay for a teacher since his stable hands have their duties. But you must accept his decision if it will be too inconvenient."

"No inconvenience at all."

All three swiveled toward the doorway.

Adolphus, his hair slightly mussed from his morning ride, stood there in virile masculine elegance, one shoulder propped on the doorframe.

Her heart turned over, as it did every time she saw him these days.

"I was looking for you, Rémi and Nathalie." Straightening, he winked at the children. "I have a surprise for you in the stables. While you are there, we can decide which horse you would like to ride."

"Truly, my lord?" Rémi stared at Adolphus as if he were an angel descended from heaven.

"Truly, son."

Rémi rushed to Adolphus and threw his arms around

his waist. Not to be left out, Nathalie too hurried to show her appreciation by hugging him.

He returned the children's embrace, and emotion clogged Aurelie's throat.

Adolphus raised his eyes to meet hers, and the warmth and promise in those brown depths made her heart turn over. With a final pat on their backs, he turned the children toward the door. "Run along to the stables. We'll be along in a few minutes."

After an approving nod from Aurelie, they grabbed hands and exited the room, just short of a run.

"That was very kind of you, Adol—my lord." Aurelie still struggled to address him properly. In her mind and heart, he was Adolphus.

"I've told you before you may call me by my given name." His smile crinkled the corners of his eyes as he approached.

"It would give the other servants the wrong impression." She cast a swift glance toward the open door. Though in truth, she suspected the other domestics already believed her relationship with Adolphus was something more than a mere housekeeper.

He roved his gaze over her navy-blue gown. "Too severe for your coloring, but I suppose you think it appropriate for your position."

"It is."

She must look the part, even if she was likely

England's youngest housekeeper. Thank goodness, she'd acted as Gaston's hostess and oversaw the running of his household after his wife died giving birth to Rémi. She wasn't totally adrift carrying out her duties at Hawkshead Court.

This gown, one of several Adolphus had commissioned for her in Lymington, as well as clothing for the children and Aunt Marie, was simple yet serviceable. Perfect for someone of her new station.

Adolphus drew abreast of her, and the intensity in his eyes made her pulse flutter.

"You've done a wondrous job with the house, Aurelie."

He insisted on addressing her by her given name, the obstinate man.

"It's a magnificent home."

She still wasn't certain why he'd given her the housekeeper's position, but she wasn't about to look a gift horse in the mouth.

He glanced around the room before settling that unnerving gaze upon her again. He lowered his focus to her mouth.

Lord, how Aurelie wanted him to kiss her.

Then as if he'd heard her unspoken prayer, ever so slowly, Adolphus lowered his head until his mouth touched hers. Blissfully sweet and tender, it wasn't enough.

She grasped his lapels and angled her head in a silent plea for more. More of him, his kisses, his touch.

With a satisfied growl deep in his throat, he pulled her into his embrace, one hand low on her spine, just above her buttocks, and the other framing her face so she could not escape. When his mouth covered hers this time, it was with possessiveness and ravenous hunger.

She opened to him, thrilled at the sensations he stirred. She'd wanted this for so long, but until this moment, she didn't know this was what she'd yearned for.

A noise in the hallway made her jerk away from him.

With the back of her hand against her still throbbing lips, she stared at him.

What had Aurelie done?

She'd not only allowed Adolphus to kiss her, but with her brazen behavior, she'd insisted he do so because she loved him so much.

Fool. Fool. Fool.

It didn't matter if Aurelie had wanted him to kiss her and she'd wanted to kiss him. She was his servant, and she needed this position. That meant she must keep her growing feelings to herself. Hide them. Camouflage them. Stuff them in a corner or the rubbish bin. Make certain this never happened again.

"I'm sorry—"

"Shh." He put a finger to her lips. "Don't ever be sorry for enjoying our kisses."

"It's wrong. I am grateful for my position. You know I am. But I told you I cannot be more than a housekeeper."

He chuckled and attempted to draw her hand through his elbow, but she shook her head, and he released her.

"I've never asked you to be anything else." He winked and waggled his eyebrows as he drew her toward the door. "*Yet.*"

"Adolphus," she warned, giving him what she hoped was a stern look but which probably was merely adoration. "You cannot say things like that. Someone might overhear."

"I'm but teasing, Aurelie."

Was he?

"Come with me. I want to show you the surprise I found for the children today." Mischief twinkled in his eyes as they approached the entrance.

Withers, the butler, proceeded with measured steps across the parquet floor to open the door for them. In the fortnight since retaining him as a butler, he'd never strayed from his precise steps. Aurelie doubted any force on earth could compel the servant to walk faster or slower.

As Aurelie followed Withers, she kept a respectful distance from Adolphus.

"We're going to the stables, Withers." With a spring in his step, Adolphus grinned. "Don't suppose you'd care to join us? There's a surprise there for the children."

"I am aware, sir, and have the footmen preparing even

as we speak." Though he spoke without emotion, humor glinted in his hazel eyes. "I shall respectfully refrain from accompanying you. Horseflesh makes me sneeze and my eyes water."

Adolphus took her elbow as they descended the front steps. "What is this secret that isn't a secret at all if Withers knows about it?"

"You'll have to wait and see." Adolphus looked entirely too proud of himself. "I think you'll be pleased. I also have the perfect little Egyptian Arabian mare for you."

"Oh, no." She shook her head while sending him an apologetic smile. "Horses and I do not get along. I'm fine with the children learning to ride, but I'll just observe, thank you."

"Why, Aurelie Lemieux. I didn't think you were afraid of anything." Adolphus's gentle teasing eased her embarrassment. "You are brave and stalwart and stoic."

She tried not to be pleased with the compliment, but inside, she glowed at his praise.

"I detest spiders and thunderstorms." Aurelie gave a little self-depreciative shrug. "I'm also not fond of snakes, mice, and beetles."

He laughed as he firmly took her hand and placed it in the crook of his elbow.

After glancing at the house and assuring herself no one watched them, she left it there.

"I rather dislike spiders myself." He swiftly perused the area and bent near, whispering conspiratorially, "I do not like ram sheep. As a child, one butted me in the bottom. That blasted thing chased me to the fence and tried to climb up after me."

Picturing a ram chasing his proper little self made Aurelie laugh. "And I thought peers were impervious to all things. *Non?*"

"No more than any other man." His sudden seriousness made her glance at him sharply.

His focus fixed on the stables, though a muscle flexed in his jaw.

As they entered the building, excited chatter and delighted childish laughter filtered from a nearby stall. Horse sweat, hay, the sweet aroma of mash, leather, and horse manure met Aurelie's nostrils.

She gave Adolphus a curious look. "What have you done?"

"Aunt Aurelie!" Nathalie carefully picked her way toward Aurelie with a wriggling bundle of brown and white in her arms that had the propensity to lick her face every two or three steps.

Rémi followed, walking just as carefully and carrying a similar wiggling package with such reverence he might be holding a holy relic.

"Puppies." Tears sprang to Aurelie's eyes as she put

her hands out to touch their silky coats. "You found them puppies."

Surely this was another sign that they were to stay and make Hawkshead Court their home.

"Aren't they precious?" Nathalie nuzzled her pup. "Mine's a girl, and Rémi's is a boy."

What else would they be?

"We can keep them, can't we, Aunt Aurelie?" Rémi's expression held hope and fear.

"Of course, you may." Aurelie couldn't stop smiling. "Withers said the footmen are already preparing the house for them."

A jab of recrimination stabbed her. A diligent housekeeper ought to have known that detail.

Still, how could she brood on her neglect when Adolphus had made another dream come true for the children?

How easy it would be to let herself show him her love.

Foolish and idiotic and imprudent, but oh, so easy.

His expression tender, Adolphus nodded to a stable hand carrying a third puppy, this one all black.

"For you, Aurelie. It's a girl."

She couldn't hold back the dratted tears as she accepted the warm, sweet-smelling little imp who promptly nibbled her chin.

A puppy.

Adolphus had a puppy for her too.

The dear, sweet man.

Any part of her heart that had remained Aurelie's promptly betrayed her and flew the few inches to reside with him.

"*Merci*," she managed through her tight throat. "I shall name her Belle. It means beautiful girl, and she is such a beautiful little girl."

Belle licked her chin, and Aurelie giggled.

This gift meant he intended for them to stay, bringing her no small amount of relief and joy.

He scratched his jaw. "I do wonder what Antoinette will think."

Aurelie and the children exchanged horrified glances before bursting into laughter.

"I think we can assume she will loathe them." Aurelie rubbed her face in the puppy's soft fur. "Children, take your puppies to the house. Do be careful where you step. Ask Withers where they will be kept and start thinking about what you will name them."

"I already know," Nathalie announced proudly. "She is Princess."

"I haven't decided." Rémi looked between Aurelie and Adolphus. "He must have a proper name. Something befitting him."

"There is no rush, Rémi." Adolphus patted the pup's head and received a sharp nip to his fingertips as a reward. "He's a little rascal."

Nathalie and Rémi dutifully marched ahead, talking excitedly between kissing their pups and giggling when their new pets nibbled their fingers.

Snuggling Belle, Aurelie savored the moment, one of the happiest of her life, and it was thanks to Adolphus.

"Did I overstep again, Aurelie?"

She glanced up to find Adolphus watching her, something akin to nervousness in his dark eyes.

"Oh, very much so."

His features tightened.

Placing her hand on his chest, she permitted a shy smile. "I'm glad you did."

Then she stood on tiptoe and pressed her lips to his, and she tasted bliss once more until Belle decided she'd had enough of being ignored and bit her chin.

Aurelie didn't know what to make of this shift in her relationship with Adolphus, but she'd take it one day at a time and see where it led.

NINETEEN

Hawkshead Court Study

THE NEXT AFTERNOON

Adolphus scratched his ear as he read a letter from his mother in the still, slightly stuffy study at the back of the house. Her excitement over Lucius's nuptials and the possibility of grandchildren fairly oozed off the pages. If Adolphus had his way and the Good Lord smiled upon him, he hoped to share news of another wedding soon.

Mother said she and Father wanted to visit next week with Althelia.

Naturally, when he'd arranged to bring his horses to Hawkshead Court, his family wanted to know why. He'd finally told them about his cottage in Lymington and his business ventures there. It had been important to him to find success on his own and not rely upon the duchy's wealth or title.

A *tap tap tap* near the open window drew his attention.

His daily visitor, a great spotted woodpecker, hammered the oak tree, establishing its territory. The poor little fellow was a bit late in the season and probably wouldn't find a mate this year.

A rustling outside the door revealed Aurelie had arrived with the tea tray he'd requested. Normally, Withers delivered tea, but Adolphus said he needed to discuss something of importance regarding Hawkshead Court with her, and would she mind bringing a tray when she came for the four o'clock appointment?

Leaving the door ajar, Aurelie slipped into the room with an inherent grace and sent him a shy smile.

"Do you want the tray on your desk or the table?" She glanced at the mahogany table before a burgundy leather sofa with matching tufted chairs on either side.

"The table, I think."

She glided forward, today's gown—a deep rich green that made her look like a wood sprite—swishing about her trim ankles. "Shall I pour?"

She'd make a marvelous duchess.

Of more import, she'd make him the perfect wife.

"No. Not yet." Adolphus came from behind the desk and gestured for her to sit. "Please sit."

The merest hint of wariness caused the corners of her eyes to flex, but she sank gracefully onto the sofa and demurely folded her hands. "You said you needed to speak with me regarding something important?"

Where to start and not botch his carefully hatched plan? He glanced at the partially open door. Should he close it before proposing? What were the chances that someone would overhear?

Not likely.

After yesterday's soul-searing kiss in the green salon and Aurelie's impromptu show of affection in the stables, he'd decided it was time to act. Heaven help him if he'd calculated wrong, and it was too soon.

Adolphus grazed his fingertips over his chin as he also sat. "Yes. I did wish to speak with you."

Aurelie regarded him, her gray eyes clear and guileless. A man could drown in the depths of those eyes. "As you know, I shall inherit the dukedom when my father dies."

No time soon, hopefully. May Father live to the ripe old age of a hundred.

Tensing, she gave him a cautious nod and clasped her hands until the knuckles showed white. "Of course."

"There are expectations of me as the next duke. I must marry and provide an heir."

Devil take it.

He sounded like a pompous ponce. The speech he'd rehearsed had fled from his head, and he'd fallen back on stiff formality.

Aurelie had gone perfectly still, watching him like a trapped animal regarded a predator.

Children's laughter and excited yapping floated into the study from somewhere inside the house.

Adolphus changed tactics. Never had he been this inept at speaking.

"I have found the woman I wish to marry. She's everything I could want in a duchess. Kind. Intelligent. She loves children. She makes me happier than I ever believed possible."

Aurelie swallowed and averted her gaze, the picture of despondency. "I'm very happy for you."

Her French accent thickened as Adolphus recognized it did when she was upset.

He almost laughed, for she sounded like she'd just delivered condolences rather than felicitations.

Though he'd been determined not to muck this up, it seems he'd done just that. Perhaps a more direct approach was in order.

"Yes, well. I haven't proposed yet." He rubbed his nose, feeling more insecure and uncertain than he could ever recall. His future, his happiness depended on the outcome. "You see, I don't know how she feels about me. I think she might hold me in warm regard, but I'm unsure if she loves me."

Her expression softened, and she roved those soft gray eyes over his face. "I'm sure she's quite taken with you too."

Adolphus certainly hoped so.

"May I...?" Aurelie cleared her throat and darted him a brief glance. "May I inquire what that means for my position?"

She still didn't understand. Always before, when they'd spoken, she'd been so perceptive that she practically read his thoughts.

Why couldn't he just say the words?

Take a chance of being rejected?

Why must he beat around the bush?

Because he was terrified he might be wrong.

And if Aurelie didn't love him and didn't want to marry him, what would he do? To think, mere weeks ago, he'd been furious when he thought she plotted to snare him in marriage, and now he was desperate to make her his wife.

He poured tenderness and adoration into his half-smile.

"You shan't be my housekeeper any longer because—"

"I thought as much." Not giving him a chance to finish, she turned pain-filled eyes upon him, her features ravaged. "*Mon Dieu*! Why bother bringing us here, giving us puppies, if you only meant to turn us out in a matter of weeks?"

She trembled with suppressed anger and shock. "What will we do?"

She looked so lost and forlorn that Adolphus's heart nearly broke.

He took her hand and brought it to his lips.

"Aurelie, my darling. Forgive me. I should've been frank from the beginning. Please don't be upset. It's you who has made me happy. You who has shown me that I don't have to settle for a marriage of convenience. Above all else, I want to marry you if *you'll* have me."

She blinked. Then blinked again.

"*Me*?" Her lower lip trembled, and tears filled her eyes. "It's *me* you want to marry?"

Tears burned in Adolphus's eyes too. "Yes, my love. More than anything I have ever wanted before."

"But we are of different stations." Her watery gaze searched his. "What will people say?"

"Do you love me, Aurelie?"

He held his breath. No response had ever mattered as much.

Adoration softened her delicate features. "I do. I have for so long. Since that night in the garden when my midnight marquess shared his hopes and dreams with me."

Thank God, his soul shouted in celebration.

"And I love you with such a consuming, enduring love. I don't care what anyone else thinks." He cupped her face and grazed his lips across hers. "That is all that matters today, tomorrow, and in our future. Our love will carry us through whatever comes our way."

"Are you positive?" she whispered. "What will your family say?"

He chuckled. "They will be delighted. I promise you. Especially my brother Lucius who told me to get my arse back to Lymington and give you a chance."

She gave him a tremulous smile. "I think I'll like your brother."

"I ask you again, Aurelie Lemieux, keeper of my heart and my soulmate, will you marry me? The man. Not a lord. Not a future duke. Marry me, the man?"

The smile blossoming across her face lit the room with its brilliance. "I shall because it is the man that I love. Not your title. Not your wealth. Not your possessions. The man who makes my heart leap with joy and fills it with so much love, I want to weep."

He pulled her onto his lap. "I'm overjoyed, my darling."

"Kiss me, Adolphus."

And he did most thoroughly.

EPILOGUE

Aboard the Schooner Midnight Rendezvous
The Mediterranean Sea near Port di Napoli

SEPTEMBER 1826 ~ HALF PAST NINE IN THE MORNING

Aurelie stood near the *Midnight Rendezvous'* gleaming rail, excitedly taking in the bustle as the deckhands prepared the ship for disembarking. Though slightly wrinkled from being confined in her traveling trunk, the smart pink traveling ensemble she'd saved for her first day in Italy boosted her confidence.

This marchioness business took a great deal of getting accustomed to.

The ship had performed splendidly on her maiden voyage, and Aurelie was pleasantly surprised that her stomach didn't plague her after the first two days at sea.

Adolphus, a born sailor, hadn't suffered any seasickness and, when not at her side, could be found chatting with the captain, first mate, or a sailor. The *Midnight Rendezvous* crew seemed flattered that the ship's owner took such personal interest in them and the vessel.

Touring Italy and Greece.

She couldn't think of a better way to begin their life together.

Adolphus joined her at the rail and wrapped an arm around her waist, pulling her to his side. "It's quite something, isn't it? Even more glorious than I'd anticipated."

Awe peppered his tone as he couldn't conceal his eagerness to explore either.

The noise, smells, and chaos added to the excitement.

"*Oui.* It is." She sent him a sideways glance and a broad smile. "I'm so glad we came."

He dropped a kiss on her forehead. "I am too, my adorable persistent, won't-take-no-for-an-answer wife. We must take at least one journey a year." He shook his head. "No, two."

Heart overflowing with love and happiness, Aurelie laughed. "Is this the same man who said he could never travel?"

"You showed me the error of my ways." Adolphus

tipped her chin up with his forefinger and brushed a reverent kiss over her mouth.

Aurelie ought to scold him for kissing her in full view of everyone, but she didn't mind, so why pretend affront?

At first, he'd balked at taking a honeymoon outside of England. He had duties. Responsibilities. And so on. Even as Adolphus argued those points, wistfulness had filled his dark brown eyes and lowered the timbre of his voice.

One evening after they'd made love and she lay upon his chest, she'd cupped his face with one hand, rubbing her thumb over the sensitive spot near his ear.

He'd fairly purred in pleasure.

"Adolphus, *mon cher*. The Lord gives us but one life to live. Do you really think He wishes you to relinquish your greatest desires? Especially since you have the means of achieving them?"

"It would be selfish, rash, irresponsible," he insisted.

All well-rehearsed excuses she'd heard before.

"Your father wants you to travel. He told you so himself." She'd pushed herself onto her elbows and searched his dear features. "What is the worst that could happen?"

He'd trailed a finger down her spine, causing a delicious little tremor. "I don't come home, and Leonidas inherits."

"God forbid any such thing." Aurelie had wrapped

her arms around him and held him tightly. She kissed his chest, grinning when the curly hair tickled her nose. "But that could happen in England too, couldn't it?"

He'd pressed his lips to the top of her head and, voice gruff, said, "You know it could."

"So?" She'd pressed his ribs. "Live life, Adolphus. All of it. Take every opportunity that comes your way and be grateful. You've been blessed. Don't throw those gifts away."

And, at last, he'd acquiesced.

Now leaning into his solid strength, as they observed the bustling wharf below, Aurelie savored his sandalwood and spice scent and his muscular body molded next to hers. Her cheeks heated as she recalled that naked muscular body and how her beloved husband awakened her this morning.

"It is magnificent." Aurelie inhaled the pungent air. "Next time, we should bring the children."

"Not those naughty dogs, though." Adolphus tried to sound stern, but he loved the dogs as much as she and the children did. The trio had captivated the servants too, and even Antoinette tolerated their presence with surprising grace. "Rascal chewed up another pair of my boots."

Rémi had quickly decided that Racal was a perfect name for his energetic pup.

She giggled behind her hand. "Oh, dear."

Nothing was safe from the puppies' needle-like teeth.

"I suppose we have Antoinette to thank for our happiness," Aurelie mused, observing the bustle on the wharf. "If she hadn't been such a naughty puss, we might never have met."

"I'll thank her with a treat when we return home." Adolphus pressed a kiss to her temple. "*Thank you*, my darling."

Canting her head, Aurelie met his tender gaze. That this man loved her and had chosen her to be his wife still left her in awe. "For what?"

"For making me realize I am more than a marquess and a future duke. My title and position do not define me." He tucked her arm into his elbow and turned her toward the gangplank. "And for agreeing to marry me. *That*, my darling, was and will always be my greatest desire.

He kissed her. "I love you, Aurelie."

He truly did.

Happy tears pricked her eyes, but Aurelie refused to cry. Not today.

"And I love you so very much, Adolphus."

He steered her toward the opening in the rail, where a crew member stood to assist them onto the gangplank if needed. "Shall we embark on our first great adventure, my darling?"

She corrected him as they stepped onto the gangway. "Our second adventure, dearest."

He gave her a questioning look as they descended.

"Marrying was our first."

"Indeed it was, and when we are old, we will tell our grandchildren how we met over a brick wall in a small seashore town in England and fell in love."

I hope you enjoyed
THE MIDNIGHT MARQUESS
and following the romantic journey
of Aurelie and Adolphus.
If you'd like to leave a review
please scan the following QR Code

SCAN HERE TO LEAVE A REVIEW FOR
"THE MIDNIGHT MARQUESS"

*Keep reading for a **FREE PREVIEW** of*
HOLLY, MISTLETOE, AND MIDNIGHT SNOW
Book 4
Chronicles of the Westbrook Brides Series...

FROM THE DESK OF COLLETTE CAMERON®

I adored researching Lymington, England. The little tidbits I share about the township are historical facts, even the snippet about the local church storing smugglers' contraband. There wasn't an official fire brigade in Lymington until the late 1800s, but I took artistic liberty created a volunteer force.

The reference to a prior French king seizing properties and assets was King Philip IV. Rumored to owe the Knights Templars money, he conspired with the Pope to accuse the templars of heresy rather than pay the significant debt. I mentioned the Plough as a constellation Adolphus could recognize. That constellation is known as the Big Dipper in the United States and Canada.

Hugs,

Collette Cameron®

Holly, Mistletoe, & Midnight Snow
CHRONICLES of the Westbrook Brides
USA Today Bestselling Author
COLLETTE CAMERON

FREE PREVIEW

BOOK 4 ~ CHRONICLES OF THE WESTBROOK
BRIDES SERIES

HOLLY, MISTLETOE, AND MIDNIGHT SNOW©

Landford Park Ballroom

19 DECEMBER, 1826 ~ LATE AFTERNOON

Why did I let Leonidas Westbrook talk me
into this ludicrous farce?

Taking in the ostentatious manor—
every window glowing with a warm welcome—and the
immaculate grounds dusted with snowfall as if God
Himself thought the tableau needed a sprinkling of festiv-
ity, Owen Lockington swore inwardly.

I've lost my everlasting bloody mind.

Slinging a battered satchel over his shoulder before
dragging an equally dilapidated leather valise from the
hackneyed coach's interior, he caught sight of his humble,

less-than-fashionable attire and his scuffed boots, badly in need of a good polish.

I'm as out of place as feather dusters at a duel.

A crooked, self-deprecating grin skewed his mouth upward on one side as he gave a contemptuous shake of his head.

Nothing new there.

How long had it been since he felt he belonged anywhere?

Since his mother had been alive.

Dour, pensive, and resembling his mother's large, rough Gaelic tribal ancestors, Owen had never fit in. It was a wonder, in truth, that he and Leonidas had become such good friends at university. A friendship that had prevailed for over a decade now, though they seldom saw each other.

When they did, however, they resumed their acquaintance as if no time had passed.

A good-sized male Dalmatian pranced over to inspect the new arrival. After thoroughly sniffing Owen's feet and calves, the chap lifted his head for a pet.

"I've passed muster, have I?" Owen scratched behind the dog's solid black ears.

The dog thumped his thick tail thrice before trotting off, sniffing several bushes, and marking his territory along the way.

Unease scraping sharp talons the length of his spine,

Owen once more skimmed his gaze over the stately mansion, smoke winding lazily skyward from multiple chimneys. Yet rather than turn around on his next breath, leap into the cold, smelly conveyance, and order the burly driver to make haste back to the village as common sense admonished, Owen sprinted up the steps.

At least this year, he wouldn't spend Christmas with only a bottle of brandy and a book for company, as he'd done for nearly a decade.

Leonidas had assured Owen that his parents, the Duke and Duchess of Latham, would welcome a guest for the holiday. Wholly out of character, Owen had accepted the invitation from his only close friend after running into him in London.

He already regretted his impulsive decision, but there was dashed little he could do now. Unless he stole a horse from the stables or walked, his chance for escape rumbled down the gravel drive, leaving dual ribbons in the glistening snow.

Filling his lungs with crisp winter air, he braced his shoulders.

A week at Hefferwickshire House was survivable, even for a social outcast such as himself.

He'd trimmed his hair this morning, and the unfashionable, unruly sable locks only brushed his collar now. He'd even deemed to shave his beard, lest the servants think him a vagabond and direct him to the back of the house for a crust of bread.

Sighing, Owen rapped upon the entrance with his forefinger's knuckle and veered a glance heavenward. The gray, lackluster sky and dusky horizon portending nightfall and, perchance, more snow matched his sour mood.

The door flew open. As if Leonidas had peered out a window awaiting Owen's arrival, his oldest friend stood there grinning like a baboon.

"Lockington! You actually came." He pumped Owen's hand. "I'm delighted! Flabbergasted but sincerely delighted."

"Do you generally answer the door, Westbrook?" Owen asked drolly, stepping inside. The splendor slapped him in the face like a frigid arctic wind.

Hefferwickshire's exterior merely hinted at the interior's opulence.

Seasonal greenery with gold and scarlet ribbons adorned the elegant entry, filling the air with a pleasant pine aroma. A stunning Spode porcelain urn overflowing with cedar, holly, and fir stood majestically atop a marble-topped rosewood half table. Kissing boughs, heavy with white mistletoe berries, hung suspended from doorways by silver and gold ribbons, awaiting stolen kisses.

His heels echoed hollowly on the black and white Italian marble as he ventured forward a few more steps, unable to keep from craning his neck and gawking like a child at a circus.

Unlike many aristocrats, Leonidas wasn't a pretentious prick and had never hinted at his family's wealth. The manor fairly oozed grandeur and opulence, but his friend stood there, looking for all the world like an ordinary chap happy to see his long-time friend.

Yes, indeed. I'm as out of my element as an engorged tick on King George IV's broad arse.

"Simms, our butler, is dealing with a situation in the kitchen. A kerfuffle regarding too much sampling of brandied fruit and tipsy maids. I believe there might've been tossing of said fruit involved." Still smiling as if Leonidas had triumphed in a *coup d'état*, he shook his dark head. "I admit, I had doubts, and I swear a couple of minutes ago, you contemplated diving back in that miserable excuse of a coach."

Leonidas jutted his chin toward the rickety equipage trundling down the drive before turning and disappearing onto the main track.

So, he *had* been watching Owen.

"I did, in truth." A raspy chuckle escaped Owen. "But then I remembered you mentioned your cook made exceptional cinnamon buns, gingerbread men, Christmas pudding, and sugared almonds." He patted his flat stomach with his free hand. "I do like my sweets."

"Aye, I recall that about you, yet you never appear to

gain weight. Must be your gargantuan size." Leonidas stepped farther into the grand entry. He gave a mischievous wink. "I'd say the brandied fruit ought to be quite the thing too."

"Don't believe I've ever had the pleasure." Owen shifted his bags.

"Come in and meet the family," Leonidas urged. "You're just in time for afternoon tea, and Mrs. Tastespotting, our cook, made several special holiday biscuits and tarts. This time of year, there are always extra treats to sample."

Mama only ever made shortbread during the holidays —a tribute to her Scot's ancestry and a testimony to Beauford's parsimony. Though the earl paid their basic expenses, he hadn't been generous with his purse. They'd managed by skimping and economizing, habits that Owen had carried into adulthood and still served him well.

Speaking over his shoulder, Leonidas shut the door with a firm *snick*. "We don't eat supper until eight o'clock, which isn't typical country hours, so tea is generally quite substantial. I'm sure you're famished after the journey."

As Owen ate when he felt hungry and had never adhered to specific hours for mealtimes, he lifted a shoulder. Regardless, his stomach did gnaw rather persistently at his backbone at the moment. A sensation he'd grown accustomed to since hunger was a regular bedfellow.

Efficient, polite footmen in crisp crimson and gold

livery took his two shoddy bags, treating the baggage with the reverence and consideration worthy of His Majesty's luggage.

"Perhaps I ought to tidy up a jot first." Owen hadn't a doubt the servants' crisp livery was far costlier than his rumpled suit. However, the clothing the servants presently toted upstairs was only slightly better than the travel suit he wore.

He'd never cared about current fashion, fancy waistcoats, expensive fabric, and assuredly didn't give two farthings whether he tied his cravat in a waterfall or a ballroom knot.

"Nonsense. No need to change." Leonidas shook his dark head again, still wearing that infuriatingly pleased-with-himself smile. "We don't stand on formality around here, and you are expressly forbidden to address me or my brothers as *my lord*." He gave an exaggerated shudder. "Besides, Grandmama doesn't like her tea to grow cold."

Affection and a trace of awe leached into Leonidas's voice when he mentioned his grandmother.

Owen never knew his grandmothers.

Rubbing his nose, Leonidas chuckled. "She's quite an eccentric old bird. I probably ought to have warned you. I beg you, don't be surprised at anything she might say or ask. She's quite beyond the pale and enjoys shocking people."

"Your parents are a *duke and duchess.*" Owen quirked a sardonic eyebrow and clasped his hands behind his back. A practice he'd developed in order to do something with his oversized hands. "I find it hard to fathom that they don't strictly abide by all decorum. You are positive they won't take exception to me addressing you with such familiarity?"

"Not at all, and I think you'll be pleasantly surprised, my friend." Leonidas slapped Owen's shoulder. "My parents are genuinely warm people. You've nothing to fear or be ashamed of. No need to worry about their approval and all that trite rot that the ponces in London are so fond of."

Leonidas knew Owen's scandalous origins, that he was the by-blow of a governess and an earl.

Though, to the Earl of Beauford's credit, he'd done the honorable thing and acknowledged his bastard son by paying for Owen's upbringing and education. No more than he ought to have done after seducing an innocent girl and then dismissing her when her condition became known to the countess, who had only ever managed to produce three daughters.

How that circumstance had aggravated the old codger.

Beauford finally had his son, but Owen would never —could never—be his heir.

"I have the one thing Beauford covets above all else."

Mouth bent into a poignant smile, Mama would hug Owen before ruffling his thick, unruly hair. "*You*, my precious boy." She'd kissed his cheek, the essence of lavender wafting from her pale skin. "And I love you above all else."

Nevertheless, the shame of her circumstances and the ostracism by her family had shattered her spirit, and she'd died just after his seventeenth birthday, leaving him alone in the world where bastards were as numerous as rats and mice and treated with the same abhorrence as the detested vermin.

Owen had rebuffed Beauford's overtures to visit and become acquainted with the man. He hadn't shed a tear when the old sod died four years ago, ironically or perhaps aptly, on Owen's fourth and twentieth birthday.

The inheritance he'd bequeathed Owen still sat in a bank account in London, untouched. Owen didn't even know how much the seducer of innocents had left him. He didn't give a blacksmith's damn how much it was.

He didn't want his sire's money.

Although if he didn't find the investors he sought to restart the coal mine in Workington that Owen had unexpectedly inherited from his maternal grandfather, then necessity might force him to accept the bequeathment.

Bitterness burned the back of his throat.

That thought, a very real possibility, galled him to his marrow.

He must find another way.

In truth, because of how the Lockingtons had treated Mama, he initially hadn't wanted his grandfather's mine either. He supposed that made him the worst sort of hypocrite, accepting one inheritance while shunning the other.

"Leonidas? Grandmama sent me to fetch you. She vows her tea grows cold but won't take a sip until you return." A pretty girl strode into the foyer, her auburn hair streaked with fire and sunshine tied back with a pink ribbon across her crown. She wore a shirt a shade darker than her hair ribbon, and trousers covered her impossibly long legs tucked into men's boots.

If his life had depended on it, Owen couldn't have torn his attention away from the arresting vixen.

She slid to a stop, her blue, blue eyes round as dinnerplates and her full berry-red mouth parting.

"Lord have mercy and blow me over with a feather. You are quite the biggest man I have ever laid eyes upon."

***I hope you enjoyed this FREE PREVIEW of
HOLLY, MISTLETOE, AND MIDNIGHT SNOW
Book 4***

Chronicles of the Westbrook Brides Series.
If you'd like to keep reading
please scan the following QR Code.

SCAN HERE TO GET "HOLLY, MISTLETOE, AND MIDNIGHT SNOW"

GIGGLES ARE GUARANTEED

If you love to chat about all things romance-book related and enjoy taking part in fun and engaging live events, contests, and giveaways join **Collette's Chèris VIP Reader Group,** my exclusive private book group on Facebook.

Giggles are guaranteed!

Hope to see you there,

Collette Cameron®

Please scan the following QR Code to join:

DUKES COME CALLING
A Sensual Marriage of Convenience
Regency Historical Romance

FOR THE LOVE OF AN EARL (Wicked Earls' Club)

A Humorous Aristocrat and Wallflower

Regency Romance Adventure

Earl of Wainthorpe — Book 1

Earl of Scarborough — Book 2

Earl of Keyworth — Book 3

Earl of Renshaw — Book 4

HEART OF A SCOT

A Passionate Enemies to Lovers

Scottish Highlander Historical Mystery

Romance Adventure

To Love a Highland Laird — Book 1

To Redeem a Highland Rogue — Book 2

To Seduce a Highland Scoundrel — Book 3

To Woo a Highland Warrior — Book 4

To Enchant a Highland Earl — Book 5

To Defy a Highland Duke — Book 6

To Marry a Highland Marauder — Book 7

To Bargain with a Highland Buccaneer — Book 8

A Christmas Kiss for the Highlander — Book 9

HIGHLAND HEATHER ROMANCING A SCOT: CASTLE BRIDES

A Passionate Enemies to Lovers Second Chance Scottish Highlander Mystery Romance

Heart of a Highlander — Prequel

The Viscount's Vow — Book 1

The Highlander's Heiress — Book 2

The Earl's Enticement — Book 3

Triumph and Treasure — Book 4

Virtue and Valor — Book 5

Heartbreak and Honor — Book 6

Scandal's Splendor — Book 7

Passion and Plunder — Book 8

Wishes and Wonder — Book 9

A Yuletide Highlander — Book 10

SECRETS OF SCANDALOUS LADIES

A Romantic Class Difference Forced Proximity

Regency Romance with Aristocrats

A Lady, A Kish, A Christmas Wish — Book 1

No Lady for the Lord — Book 2

Love Lessons for a Lady — Book 3

His One and Only Lady — Book 4

Never a Proper Lady — Book 5

Lady Tempts a Rogue — Book 6

THE CULPEPPER MISSES

A Humorous Wallflower Family Saga

Regency Romantic Comedy

THE HONORABLE ROGUES®
A Second Chance Redeemable Rogue
and Wallflower Regency Romance

ABOUT THE AUTHOR

USA Today Bestselling author Collette Cameron® is renowned for her captivating, humorous, and heart-warming Scottish and Regency historical romance novels. With over 65 published titles, over 1.4 million books sold around the world, and multiple writing awards to her credit, Collette is a well-known author in the world of historical romance. Readers love her witty and relatable characters including daring rogues, dashing scoundrels, and the strong and spirited heroines who capture their hearts. From the rugged highlands to the refined drawing rooms of Regency England, Collette's novels will transport you to another time and place, where love and adventure are just a page away.

Collette's Sweet-to-Spicy Timeless Romances® are the perfect escape for readers looking for romantic escape, poignant inspiration, engaging humor, and entertaining stories.

Based in the Pacific Northwest, Collette is surrounded by the lush greenery and rainy skies that inspire her writing. She dreams of one day splitting her time between the Pacific Northwest and Scotland. In the meantime, she indulges in her love of all things cobalt blue, dachshunds, chocolate, and of course, crafting her next historical romance.

Blue Rose Romance® LLC
PO Box 167
Scappoose, Oregon 97056 USA
collettecameron.com

If you haven't joined Collette's exclusive mailing list scan the folloing QR Code to sign up!
You'll get access to exclusive content, sneak peeks, contests, giveaways, and more...
(P.S. No spammy stuff.)

THE REGENCY ROSE®

VIP CLUB

Follow Collette on social media.
Scan the following QR Code:

collettecameron.com

COLLETTE CAMERON®

FOLLOW COLLETTE
ON
SOCIAL MEDIA